W9-BPO-665

MAN IN THE DARK

MAN IN THE DARK

PAUL AUSTER

A FRANCES COADY BOOK

HENRY HOLT AND COMPANY

NEW YORK

Henry Holt and Company, LLC
Publishers since 1866
175 Fifth Avenue
New York, New York 10010

Henry Holt® is a registered trademark of
Henry Holt and Company, LLC.

Copyright © 2008 by Paul Auster
All rights reserved.
Distributed in Canada by H. B. Fenn and Company Ltd.

Library of Congress Cataloging-in-Publication Data

Auster, Paul, 1947–
Man in the dark / Paul Auster. — 1st ed.
p. cm.
ISBN-13: 978-0-8050-8839-7
ISBN-10: 0-8050-8839-3
1. Autobiographical fiction, American. 2. Alternative histories
(Fiction), American. 3. Imaginary wars and battles—Fiction.
4. Political fiction. I. Title.
PS3551.U77M36 2008
813'.54—dc22   2007037515

First Edition 2008

Designed by Victoria Hartman

Printed in the United States of America

1 3 5 7 9 10 8 6 4 2

For David Grossman
and his wife Michal
his son Jonathan
his daughter Ruthi
and in memory of Uri

MAN IN THE DARK

I am alone in the dark, turning the world around in my head as I struggle through another bout of insomnia, another white night in the great American wilderness. Upstairs, my daughter and granddaughter are asleep in their bedrooms, each one alone as well, the forty-seven-year-old Miriam, my only child, who has slept alone for the past five years, and the twenty-three-year-old Katya, Miriam's only child, who used to sleep with a young man named Titus Small, but Titus is dead now, and Katya sleeps alone with her broken heart.

Bright light, then darkness. Sun pouring down from all corners of the sky, followed by the black of night, the silent stars, the wind stirring in the branches. Such is the routine. I have been living in this house for more than a year now, ever since they released me from the hospital. Miriam insisted that I come here, and at first it was just the two of us, along with a day nurse who looked after me when Miriam was off at work. Then, three months later, the roof fell in on Katya, and she dropped out of film school in New York and came home to live with her mother in Vermont.

His parents named him after Rembrandt's son, the little boy of the paintings, the golden-haired child in the red hat, the daydreaming pupil puzzling over his lessons, the little boy who turned into a young man ravaged by illness and who died in his twenties, just as Katya's Titus did. It's a doomed name, a name that should be banned from circulation forever. I think about Titus's death often, the horrifying story of that death, the images of that death, the pulverizing consequences of that death on my grieving granddaughter, but I don't want to go there now, I can't go there now, I have to push it as far away from me as possible. The night is still young, and as I lie here in bed looking up into the darkness, a darkness so black that the ceiling is invisible, I begin to remember the story I started last night. That's what I do when sleep refuses to come. I lie in bed and tell myself stories. They might not add up to much, but as long as I'm inside them, they prevent me from thinking about the things I would prefer to forget. Concentration can be a problem, however, and more often than not my mind eventually drifts away from the story I'm trying to tell to the things I don't want to think about. There's nothing to be done. I fail again and again, fail more often than I succeed, but that doesn't mean I don't give it my best effort.

I put him in a hole. That felt like a good start, a promising way to get things going. Put a sleeping man in a hole, and then see what happens when he wakes up and tries to crawl out. I'm talking about a deep hole in the ground, nine or ten feet deep, dug in such a way as to form a perfect circle, with sheer inner walls of dense, tightly packed earth, so hard that the surfaces have the texture of baked clay, perhaps even glass. In other words, the man in the hole will be unable to extricate himself from the hole once he opens his eyes. Unless he is equipped with a set of mountaineering tools—a hammer and metal spikes, for example, or a rope to lasso a neighboring tree—but this man has no tools, and once he regains consciousness, he will quickly understand the nature of his predicament.

And so it happens. The man comes to his senses and discovers that he is lying on his back, gazing up at a cloudless evening sky. His name is Owen Brick, and he has no idea how he has landed in this spot, no memory of having fallen into this cylindrical hole, which he estimates to be approximately twelve feet in diameter. He sits up. To his surprise, he is dressed in a soldier's uniform made of rough, dun-colored wool. A cap is on his head, and a pair of sturdy, well-worn black leather boots are on his feet, laced above the ankles with a firm double knot. There are two military stripes on each sleeve of the jacket, indicating that the uniform belongs to someone with the rank of corporal. That person might be Owen Brick, but the man in the hole, whose name is Owen Brick, cannot recall having served in an army or fought in a war at any time in his life.

For want of any other explanation, he assumes he has received a knock on the head and has temporarily lost his memory. When he puts his fingertips against his scalp and begins to search for bumps and gashes, however, he finds no traces of swelling, no cuts, no bruises, nothing to suggest that such an injury has occurred. What is it, then? Has he suffered some debilitating trauma that has blacked out large portions of his brain? Perhaps. But unless the memory of that trauma suddenly returns to him, he will have no way of knowing. After that, he begins to explore the possibility that he is asleep in his bed at home, trapped inside some supernaturally lucid dream, a dream so lifelike and intense that the boundary between dreaming and consciousness has all but melted away. If that is true, then he simply has to open his eyes, hop out of bed, and walk into the kitchen to prepare the morning coffee. But how can you open your eyes when they're already open? He blinks a few times, childishly wondering if that won't break the spell—but there is no spell to be broken, and the magic bed fails to materialize.

A flock of starlings passes overhead, entering his field of vision for five or six seconds, and then vanishes into the twilight. Brick stands up to inspect his surroundings, and as he does so he becomes aware of an object bulging in the left front pocket of his trousers. It turns out to be a wallet, his wallet, and in addition to seventy-six dollars in American money, it contains a driver's license issued by the state of New York to one Owen Brick, born June 12, 1977. This confirms what Brick already knows: that he is a man approaching thirty who lives in Jackson Heights, Queens. He also knows that he is married to a woman named Flora and that for the past seven years he has worked as a professional magician, performing mostly at children's birthday parties around the city under the stage name of the Great Zavello. These facts only deepen the mystery. If he is so certain of who he is, then how did he wind up at the bottom of this hole, dressed in a corporal's uniform no less, without papers or dog tags or a military ID card to prove his status as a soldier?

It doesn't take long for him to understand that escape is out of the question. The circular wall is too high, and when he kicks it with his boot in order to dent the surface and create some kind of foothold that would help him climb up, the only result is a sore big toe. Night is falling rapidly, and there is a chill in the air, a damp vernal chill worming itself into his body, and while Brick has begun to feel afraid, for the moment he is still more baffled than afraid. Nevertheless, he can't stop himself from calling out for help. Until now, all has been quiet around him, suggesting that he is in some remote, unpopulated stretch of countryside, with no sounds other than an occasional bird cry and the rustling of the wind. As if on command, however, as if by some skewed logic of cause and effect, the moment he shouts the word *HELP*, artillery fire erupts in the distance, and the darkening sky lights up with streaking comets of destruction. Brick hears machine guns, exploding grenades, and under it all, no doubt miles away, a dull chorus of howling human voices. This is war, he realizes, and he is a soldier in that war, but with no weapon at his disposal, no way to defend himself against attack, and for the first time since waking up in the hole, he is well and truly afraid.

The shooting goes on for more than an hour, then gradually dissipates into silence. Not long after that, Brick hears the faint sound of sirens, which he takes to mean that fire engines are rushing to buildings damaged during the assault. Then the sirens stop as well, and quiet descends on him once again. Cold and frightened as he is, Brick is also exhausted, and after pacing around the confines of his cylindrical jail until the stars appear in the sky, he stretches out on the ground and manages to fall asleep at last.

Early the next morning, he is woken by a voice calling to him from the top of the hole. Brick looks up and sees the face of a man jutting over the rim, and since the face is all he can see, he assumes the man is lying flat on his stomach.

Corporal, the man says. Corporal Brick, it's time to get moving.

Brick stands up, and now that his eyes are only three or four feet from the stranger's face, he can see that the man is a swarthy, square-jawed fellow with a two-day stubble of beard and that he is wearing a military cap identical to the one on his own head. Before Brick can protest that much as he'd like to get moving, he's in no position to do anything of the sort, the man's face disappears.

Don't worry, he hears him say. We'll have you out of there in no time.

Some moments later, there follows the sound of a hammer or iron mallet pounding on a metal object, and because the sound becomes increasingly muted with each successive blow, Brick wonders if the man isn't driving a stake into the ground.

And if it's a stake, then perhaps a length of rope will soon be attached to it, and with that rope Brick will be able to climb out of the hole. The clanging stops, another thirty or forty seconds go by, and then, just as he predicted, a rope drops down at his feet.

Brick is a magician, not a bodybuilder, and even if climbing a yard or so of rope is not an inordinately strenuous task for a healthy man of thirty, he nevertheless has a good deal of trouble hoisting himself to the top. The wall is of no use to him, since the soles of his boots keep sliding off the smooth surface, and when he tries to clamp his boots onto the rope itself, he fails to gain a secure purchase, which means that he has to rely on the strength of his arms alone, and given that his are not muscular or powerful arms, and given that the rope is made of coarse material and therefore chafes his palms, this simple operation is turned into something of a battle. When he finally nears the rim and the other man takes hold of his right hand and pulls him onto level ground, Brick is both out of breath and disgusted with himself. After such a dismal performance, he is expecting to be mocked for his ineptitude, but by some miracle the man refrains from making any disparaging comments.

As Brick struggles slowly to his feet, he notes that his rescuer's uniform is the same as his, with the single exception that there are three stripes on the sleeves of his jacket, not two. The air is dense with fog, and he has difficulty making out where he is. Some isolated spot in the country, as he suspected, but the city or town that was under attack last night is nowhere to be seen. The only things he can distinguish with any clarity are the metal stake with the rope tied around it and a mud-splattered jeep parked about ten feet from the edge of the hole.

Corporal, the man says, shaking Brick's hand with a firm, enthusiastic grip. I'm Serge Tobak, your sergeant. Better known as Sarge Serge.

Brick looks down at the man, who is a good six inches shorter than he is, and repeats the name in a low voice: Sarge Serge.

I know, Tobak says. Very funny. But the name stuck, and there's nothing I can do about it. If you can't lick 'em, join 'em, right?

What am I doing here? Brick asks, trying to suppress the anguish in his voice.

Get a grip on yourself, boy. You're fighting a war. What did you think this was? A trip to Fun World?

What war? Does that mean we're in Iraq?

Iraq? Who cares about Iraq?

America's fighting a war in Iraq. Everyone knows that.

Fuck Iraq. This is America, and America is fighting America.

What are you talking about?

Civil war, Brick. Don't you know anything? This is the fourth year. But now that you've turned up, it's going to end soon. You're the guy who's going to make it happen.

How do you know my name?

You're in my platoon, dumbbell.

And what about the hole? What was I doing down there?

Normal procedure. All new recruits come to us like that.

But I didn't sign up. I didn't enlist.

Of course not. No one does. But that's the way it is. One minute you're living your life, and the next minute you're in the war.

Brick is so confounded by Tobak's statements, he doesn't know what to say.

It's like this, the sergeant rattles on. You're the chump they've picked for the big job. Don't ask me why, but the general staff thinks you're the best man for the assignment. Maybe because no one knows you, or maybe because you have this . . . this what? . . . this bland look about you, and no one would suspect you're an assassin.

Assassin?

That's it, assassin. But I like to use the word *liberator.* Or *maker of the peace.* Whatever you want to call it, without you the war will never end.

Brick would like to run away on the spot, but because he's unarmed, he can't think of anything else to do but play along. And who am I supposed to kill? he asks.

It's not *who* so much as *what,* the sergeant replies enigmatically. We're not even sure of his name. It could be Blake. It could be Black. It could be Bloch. But we have an address, and if he hasn't slipped away by now, you shouldn't have any trouble. We'll set you up with a contact in the city, you'll go undercover, and in a few days it should all be over.

And why does this man deserve to die?

Because he owns the war. He invented it, and everything that happens or is about to happen is in his head. Eliminate that head, and the war stops. It's that simple.

Simple? You make him sound like God.

Not God, Corporal, just a man. He sits in a room all day writing it down, and whatever he writes comes true. The intelligence reports say he's racked with guilt, but he can't stop himself. If the bastard had the guts to blow his brains out, we wouldn't be having this conversation.

You're saying it's a story, that a man is writing a story, and we're all part of it.

Something like that.

And after he's killed, then what? The war ends, but what about us?

Everything goes back to normal.

Or maybe we just disappear.

Maybe. But that's the risk we have to take. Do or die, son. More than thirteen million dead already. If things go on like this much longer, half the population will be gone before you know it.

Brick has no intention of killing anyone, and the longer he listens to Tobak, the more certain he becomes that the man is a raving lunatic. For the time being, however, he has no choice but to pretend to understand, to act as if he's eager to carry out the assignment.

Sarge Serge walks over to the jeep, fetches a bulging plastic bag from the back, and hands it to Brick. Your new duds, he says, and right there in the open he instructs the magician to strip off his army uniform and put on the civilian clothes contained in the bag: a pair of black jeans, a blue oxford shirt, a red V-neck sweater, a belt, a brown leather jacket, and black leather shoes. Then he hands him a green nylon backpack filled with more clothes, shaving equipment, a toothbrush and toothpaste, a hairbrush, a .38-caliber revolver, and a box of bullets. Finally, Brick is given an envelope with twenty fifty-dollar bills in it and a slip of paper with the name and address of his contact.

Lou Frisk, the sergeant says. A good man. Go to him as soon as you get to the city, and he'll tell you everything you need to know.

What city are we talking about? Brick asks. I have no idea where I am.

Wellington, Tobak says, swiveling to his right and pointing into the heavy morning fog. Twelve miles due north. Just stay on this road, and you'll be there by the middle of the afternoon.

I'm supposed to walk?

Sorry. I'd give you a lift, but I have to go in the other direction. My men are waiting for me.

And what about breakfast? Twelve miles on an empty stomach . . .

Sorry about that, too. I was supposed to bring you an egg sandwich and a thermos of coffee, but I forgot.

Before leaving to join his men, Sarge Serge pulls the rope up from the hole, yanks the metal stake out of the ground, and tosses them into the back of the jeep. Then he climbs in behind

the steering wheel and starts the engine. Giving Brick a farewell
salute, he says: Hang in there, soldier. You don't look like much
of a killer to me, but what do I know? I'm never right about
anything.

Without another word, Tobak presses his foot on the accel-
erator, and just like that he is gone, disappearing into the fog
within a matter of seconds. Brick doesn't budge. He is both
cold and hungry, both destabilized and frightened, and for
more than a minute he just stands there in the middle of the
road, wondering what to do next. Eventually, he starts to shiver
in the frosty air. That decides it for him. He has to get his
limbs moving, to warm himself up, and so, without the faintest
notion of what lies ahead of him, he turns around, thrusts his
hands into his pockets, and begins walking toward the city.

A door has just opened upstairs, and I can hear the sound of
footsteps traveling down the hall. Miriam or Katya, I can't tell
which. The bathroom door opens and shuts; faintly, very
faintly, I detect the familiar music of pee hitting water, but
whoever has done the peeing is thoughtful enough not to flush
the toilet and risk waking the household, even if two-thirds
of its members are already awake. Then the bathroom door
opens, and once again the quiet tread down the hall and the
closing of a bedroom door. If I had to choose, I would say it was
Katya. Poor, suffering Katya, as resistant to sleep as her immo-
bilized grandfather. I would love to be able to walk up the
stairs, go into her room, and talk to her for a while. Tell some

of my bad jokes, maybe, or else just run my hand over her head until her eyes closed and she fell asleep. But I can't climb the stairs in a wheelchair, can I? And if I used my crutch, I would probably fall in the dark. Damn this idiot leg. The only solution is to sprout a pair of wings, giant wings of the softest white down. Then I'd be up there in a flash.

For the past couple of months, Katya and I have spent our days watching movies together. Side by side on the living room sofa, staring at the television set, knocking off two, three, even four films in a row, then breaking for dinner with Miriam, and once dinner has been eaten, returning to the sofa for another film or two before going to bed. I should be working on my manuscript, the memoir I promised to write for Miriam after I retired three years ago, the story of my life, the family history, a chronicle of a vanished world, but the truth is I'd rather be on the sofa with Katya, holding her hand, letting her rest her head on my shoulder, feeling my mind grow numb from the endless parade of images dancing across the screen. For over a year I went at it every day, building up a hefty pile of pages, about half the story I'd guess, perhaps a little more, but now I seem to have lost the stomach for it. Maybe it started when Sonia died, I don't know, the end of married life, the loneliness of it all, the fucking loneliness after I lost her, and then I cracked up that rented car, destroying my leg, nearly killing myself in the process, maybe that added to it as well: the indifference, the feeling that after seventy-two years on this earth, who gives a damn if I write about myself or not? It was never anything that interested me, not even when I was young, and I certainly never had any ambition to write a book. I liked to read them, that was all, to read books and then write about them afterward, but I was always a sprinter, never a long-distance man, a greyhound working on deadline for forty years, an expert at cranking out the seven-hundred-word piece, the fifteen-hundred-word piece, the twice-weekly column, the occasional magazine assignment, how many thousands of them did I vomit forth? Decades of ephemera, mounds of burned-up and recycled newsprint, and unlike most of my colleagues, I never had the slightest inclination to collect the good ones, assuming there were any, and republish them in books that no sane person would bother to read. Let my half-finished manuscript go on gathering dust for now. Miriam is hard at it, coming to the end of her biography of Rose Hawthorne, squeezing in her hours at night, on the weekends, on the days when she doesn't have to drive to Hampton to teach her courses, and for the time being maybe one writer in the house is enough.

Where was I? Owen Brick . . . Owen Brick walking down the road to the city. The cold air, the confusion, a second civil war in America. A prelude to something, but before I figure out what to do with my befuddled magician, I need a few moments to reflect on Katya and the films, since I still can't decide if this is a good thing or a bad thing. When she started ordering the DVDs through the Internet, I took it as a sign of progress, a small step in the right direction. If nothing else, it showed me that she was willing to let herself be distracted, to think about something other than her dead Titus. She's a film student, after all, training to become an editor, and when the

DVDs started pouring into the house, I wondered if she wasn't thinking about going back to school or, if not school, then furthering her education on her own. After a while, though, I began to see this obsessive movie watching as a form of self-medication, a homeopathic drug to anesthetize herself against the need to think about her future. Escaping into a film is not like escaping into a book. Books force you to give something back to them, to exercise your intelligence and imagination, whereas you can watch a film—and even enjoy it—in a state of mindless passivity. That said, I don't mean to suggest that Katya has turned herself into a stone. She smiles and sometimes even emits a small laugh during the funny scenes in comedies, and her tear ducts have frequently been active during the touching scenes in dramas. It has more to do with her posture, I think, the way she slumps back on the sofa with her feet stretched out on the coffee table, unmoving for hours on end, refusing to stir herself even to pick up the phone, showing little or no signs of life except when I'm touching or holding her. It's probably my fault. I've encouraged her to lead this flattened-out existence, and maybe I should put a stop to it—although I doubt she'd listen to me if I tried.

On the other hand, some days are better than others. Each time we finish a movie, we talk about it for a little while before Katya puts on the next one. I usually want to discuss the story and the quality of the acting, but her remarks tend to focus on the technical aspects of the film: the camera setups, the editing, the lighting, the sound, and so on. Just tonight, however, after we watched three consecutive foreign films—*Grand Illusion, The*

Bicycle Thief, and *The World of Apu*—Katya delivered some sharp and incisive comments, sketching out a theory of film-making that impressed me with its originality and acumen.

Inanimate objects, she said.

What about them? I asked.

Inanimate objects as a means of expressing human emotions. That's the language of film. Only good directors understand how to do it, but Renoir, De Sica, and Ray are three of the best, aren't they?

No doubt.

Think about the opening scenes of *The Bicycle Thief.* The hero is given a job, but he won't be able to take it unless he gets his bicycle out of hock. He goes home feeling sorry for himself. And there's his wife outside their building, lugging two heavy buckets of water. All their poverty, all the struggles of this woman and her family are contained in those buckets. The husband is so wrapped up in his own troubles, he doesn't bother to help her until they're halfway to the door. And even then, he only takes one of the buckets, leaving her to carry the other. Everything we need to know about their marriage is given to us in those few seconds. Then they climb the stairs to their apartment, and the wife comes up with the idea to pawn their bed linens so they can redeem the bicycle. Remember how violently she kicks the bucket in the kitchen, remember how violently she opens the bureau drawer. Inanimate objects, human emotions. Then we're at the pawnshop, which isn't a shop, really, but a huge place, a kind of warehouse for unwanted goods. The wife sells the sheets, and after that we see one of the workers carry their little bundle to the shelves where pawned items are stored. At first, the shelves don't seem very high, but then the camera pulls back, and as the man starts climbing up, we see that they go on and on and on, all the way to the ceiling, and every shelf and cubby is crammed full of bundles identical to the one the man is now putting away, and all of a sudden it looks as if every family in Rome has sold their bed linens, that the entire city is in the same miserable state as the hero and his wife. In one shot, Grandpa. In one shot we're given a picture of a whole society living at the edge of disaster.

Not bad, Katya. The wheels are turning . . .

It just hit me tonight. But I think I'm on to something, since I saw examples in all three films. Remember the dishes in *Grand Illusion*?

The dishes?

Right near the end. Gabin tells the German woman that he loves her, that he'll come back for her and her daughter when the war is over, but the troops are closing in now, and he and Dalio have to try to cross the border into Switzerland before it's too late. The four of them have a last meal together, and then the moment comes to say good-bye. It's all very moving, of course. Gabin and the woman standing in the doorway, the possibility that they'll never see each other again, the woman's tears as the men vanish into the night. Renoir then cuts to Gabin and Dalio running through the woods, and I'd bet money that every other director in the world would have stayed with them until the end of the film. But not Renoir. He

has the genius—and when I say *genius,* I mean the understanding, the depth of heart, the compassion—to go back to
the woman and her little daughter, this young widow who has
already lost her husband to the madness of war, and what does
she have to do? She has to go back into the house and confront
the dining room table and the dirty dishes from the meal they've
just eaten. The men are gone now, and because they're gone,
those dishes have been transformed into a sign of their absence,
the lonely suffering of women when men go off to war, and one
by one, without saying a word, she picks up the dishes and
clears the table. How long does the scene last? Ten seconds?
Fifteen seconds? No time at all, but it takes your breath away,
doesn't it? It just knocks the stuffing out of you.

You're a brave girl, I said, suddenly thinking about Titus.

Stop it, Grandpa. I don't want to talk about him. Some other
time, maybe, but not now. Okay?

Okay. Let's stick to the movies. There's still one to go. The
Indian film. I think it's the one I liked best.

That's because it's about a writer, Katya said, cracking a
brief, ironic smile.

Maybe. But that doesn't mean it isn't good.

I wouldn't have chosen it unless it was good. No junk.
That's the rule, remember? All sorts of movies, from the wacky
to the sublime, but no junk.

Agreed. But where's the inanimate object in *Apu*?

Think.

I don't want to think. It's your theory, so you tell me.

The curtains and the hairpin. A transition from one life into another, the turning point of the story. Apu has gone to the country to attend his friend's cousin's wedding. A traditional arranged marriage, and when the bridegroom shows up, he turns out to be an idiot, a blithering numskull. The wedding is called off, and the friend's cousin's parents begin to panic, afraid their daughter will be cursed for life if she doesn't get married that afternoon. Apu is asleep somewhere under the trees, not a care in the world, happy to be out of the city for a few days. The girl's family approaches him. They explain that he's the only available unmarried man, that he's the only one who can solve the problem for them. Apu is appalled. He thinks they're nuts, a bunch of superstitious country bumpkins, and refuses to go along. But then he mulls it over for a while and decides to do it. As a good deed, as an altruistic gesture, but he has no intention of taking the girl back to Calcutta with him. After the wedding ceremony, when they're finally alone together for the first time, Apu learns that this meek young woman is a lot tougher than he thought she was. I'm poor, he says, I want to be a writer, I have nothing to offer you. I know, she says, but that makes no difference, she's determined to go with him. Exasperated, flummoxed, but also moved by her resolve, Apu reluctantly gives in. Cut to the city. A carriage pulls up in front of the ramshackle building where Apu lives, and he and his bride step out. All the neighbors come to gawk at the beautiful girl as Apu leads her up the stairs to his squalid little garret. A moment later, he's called away by someone and leaves. The camera stays on the girl, alone in this strange room, this strange city, married to a man she hardly knows. Eventually, she walks to the window, which has a cruddy piece of burlap hanging over it instead of a real curtain. There's a hole in the burlap, and she looks through the hole into the backyard, where a baby in diapers is toddling along through the dust and debris. The camera angle reverses, and we see her eye through the hole. Tears are falling from that eye, and who can blame her for feeling overwrought, scared, lost? Apu reenters the room and asks her what's wrong. Nothing, she says, shaking her head, nothing at all. Then we fade to black, and the big question is: what next? What's in store for this unlikely couple who wound up marrying each other by pure accident? With a few deft and decisive strokes, everything is revealed to us in less than a minute. Object number one: the window. We fade in, it's early morning, and the first thing we see is the window the girl was looking through in the previous scene. But the ratty burlap is gone, replaced by a pair of clean checkered curtains. The camera pulls back a little, and there's object number two: potted flowers on the windowsill. These are encouraging signs, but we can't be sure what they mean yet. Domesticity, homeyness, a woman's touch, but this is what wives are supposed to do, and just because Apu's wife has carried out her duties well doesn't prove that she cares for him. The camera continues pulling back, and we see the two of them asleep in bed. The alarm clock rings, and the wife climbs out of bed as Apu groans and buries his head in the pillow. Object number three: her sari. After she gets out of bed and starts walking off, she suddenly can't move—because her clothes are tied to Apu's. Very odd. Who could have done this—and why? The expression on her face is both peeved and amused, and we instantly know that Apu was responsible. She returns to the bed, thwacks him gently on the butt, and then unties the knot. What does this moment say to me? That they're having good sex, that a sense of playfulness has developed between them, that they're really married. But what about love? They seem to be contented, but how strong are their feelings for each other? That's when object number four appears: the hairpin. The wife leaves the frame to prepare breakfast, and the camera closes in on Apu. He finally manages to open his eyes, and as he yawns and stretches and rolls around in bed, he sees something in the crevice between the two pillows. He reaches in and pulls out one of his wife's hairpins. That's the crowning moment. He holds up the hairpin and studies it, and when you look at Apu's eyes, the tenderness and adoration in those eyes, you know beyond a doubt that he's madly in love with her, that she's the woman of his life. And Ray makes it happen without using a single word of dialogue.

Same with the dishes, I said. Same with the bundle of sheets. No words.

No words needed, Katya replied. Not when you know what you're doing.

There's another thing about those three scenes. I wasn't aware of it while we were watching the films, but listening to you describe them now, it jumped right out at me.

What?

They're all about women. How women are the ones who carry the world. They take care of the real business while their hapless men stumble around making a hash of things. Or else just lie around doing nothing. That's what happens after the hairpin. Apu looks across the room at his wife, who's crouching down over a pot making breakfast, and he doesn't make a move to help her. In the same way the Italian guy doesn't notice how hard it is for his wife to carry those water buckets.

At last, Katya said, giving me a small poke in the ribs. A man who gets it.

Let's not exaggerate. I'm just adding a footnote to your theory. Your very astute theory, I might add.

And what kind of husband were you, Grandpa?

Just as distracted and lazy as the jokers in those films. Your grandmother did everything.

That's not true.

Yes, it is. When you were with us, I was always on my best behavior. You should have seen us when we were alone.

I pause for a moment to shift my position in bed, to adjust the pillow, to take a sip of water from the glass on the bedside table. I don't want to start thinking about Sonia. It's still too early, and if I let myself go now, I'll wind up brooding about her for hours. Stick to the story. That's the only solution. Stick to the story, and then see what happens if I make it to the end.

Owen Brick. Owen Brick on his way to the city of Wellington, in which state he doesn't know, in which part of the country he doesn't know, but because of the dampness and chill in the air, he suspects that he's in the north, perhaps New

England, perhaps New York State, perhaps somewhere in the Upper Midwest, and then, remembering Sarge Serge's talk about a civil war, he wonders what the fighting is about and who is fighting whom. Is it North against South again? East against West? Red against Blue? White against Black? Whatever caused the war, he tells himself, and whatever issues or ideas happen to be at stake, none of it makes any sense. How can this be America if Tobak knows nothing about Iraq? Utterly at a loss, Brick reverts to his earlier speculation that he is trapped in a dream, that in spite of the physical evidence around him, he is lying next to Flora in his bed at home.

Visibility is poor, but through the fog Brick can dimly apprehend that he is flanked by woods on both sides, that there are no houses or buildings anywhere in sight, no telephone poles, no traffic signs, no indication of human presence except the road itself, a badly paved stretch of tar and asphalt with numerous cracks and potholes, no doubt unrepaired for years. He walks on for a mile, then another mile, and still no cars drive past, no people emerge from the emptiness. Finally, after twenty minutes or so, he hears something approaching him, a clanking, whooshing sound that he is at pains to identify. Out of the fog, a man on a bicycle comes pedaling toward him. Brick raises his hand to catch the man's attention, calls out *Hello, Please, Sir,* but the cyclist ignores him and scoots on past. After a while, more people on bicycles start showing up, some riding in one direction, some in the other, but for all the notice they pay to Brick as he urges them to stop, he might as well be invisible.

Five or six miles farther down the road, signs of life begin to appear—or rather signs of former life: burned-out houses, collapsed food markets, a dead dog, several exploded cars. An old woman dressed in tattered clothes and pushing a shopping cart filled with her possessions suddenly looms up in front of him.

Excuse me, Brick says. Could you tell me if this is the road to Wellington?

The woman stops and looks at Brick with uncomprehending eyes. He notes a small tuft of whiskers sprouting from her chin, her wrinkled mouth, her gnarled, arthritic hands. Wellington? she says. Who asked you?

No one asked me, Brick says. I'm asking you.

Me? What do I have to do with it? I don't even know you.

And I don't know you. All I'm asking is if this is the road to Wellington.

The woman scrutinizes Brick for a moment and says, It'll cost you five bucks.

Five bucks for a yes or no? You must be crazy.

Everyone's crazy around here. Are you trying to tell me you're not?

I'm not trying to tell you anything. I just want to know where I am.

You're standing on a road, nitwit.

Yes, fine, I'm standing on a road, but what I want to know is if this road leads to Wellington.

Ten bucks.

Ten bucks?

Twenty bucks.

Forget it, Brick says, by now at the limit of his patience. I'll figure it out for myself.

Figure out what? the woman asks.

Instead of answering her, Brick starts walking again, and as he strides off through the fog, he hears the woman burst out laughing behind him, as if someone has just told her a good joke . . .

The streets of Wellington. It's past noon by the time he enters the city, exhausted and hungry, his feet aching from the rigors of the long trek. The sun has burned off the early morning fog, and as he wanders around in the fine, sixty-degree weather, Brick is heartened to discover that the place is still more or less intact, not some bombed-out war zone heaped with rubble and the bodies of dead civilians. He sees a number of destroyed buildings, some cratered streets, a few demolished barricades, but otherwise Wellington appears to be a functioning city, with pedestrians walking to and fro, people going in and out of shops, and no imminent threat hanging in the air. The only thing that distinguishes it from your normal American metropolis is the fact that there are no cars, trucks, or buses. Nearly everyone is moving around on foot, and those who aren't walking are mounted on bicycles. It's impossible for Brick to know yet if this is a result of a gasoline shortage or municipal policy, but he has to admit that the quiet has a pleasant effect, that he prefers it to the clamor and chaos of the streets in New York. Beyond that, however, Wellington has little to recommend it. It's a shabby, down-at-the-heels kind of place, with ugly, poorly constructed buildings, nary a tree in sight, and mounds of uncollected garbage littering the side-walks. A glum burg, perhaps, but not the out-and-out hellhole Brick was expecting.

His first order of business is to fill his stomach, but restau-rants seem to be scarce in Wellington, and he prowls around for some time before spotting a small diner on a side street off one of the main avenues. It's almost three o'clock, long past lunch hour, and the place is empty when he walks in. To his left is a counter with six vacant stools in front of it; to his right, running along the opposite wall, are four narrow booths, also vacant. Brick decides to sit at the counter. A few seconds after he settles onto one of the stools, a young woman emerges from the kitchen and slaps down a menu in front of him. She's in her mid- to late twenties, a thin, pale blonde with a weary look in her eyes and the hint of a smile on her lips.

What's good today? Brick asks, not bothering to open the menu.

More like, what do we *have* today, the waitress replies.

Oh? Well, what are the choices?

Tuna salad, chicken salad, and eggs. The tuna's from yes-terday, the chicken's from two days ago, and the eggs came in this morning. We'll cook them any way you like. Fried, scram-bled, poached. Hard, medium, soft. Whatever, however.

Any bacon or sausage? Any toast or potatoes?

The waitress rolls her eyes in mock disbelief. Dream on, honey, she says. Eggs are eggs. Not eggs with something else. Just eggs.

All right, Brick says, feeling disappointed but nevertheless trying to keep up a good front, let's go for the eggs.

How do you want them?

Let's see. . . . How do I want them? Scrambled.

How many?

Three. No, make that four.

Four? That'll cost you twenty bucks, you know. The waitress narrows her eyes, and she looks at Brick as if seeing him for the first time. Shaking her head, she adds: What are you doing in a dump like this with twenty dollars in your pocket?

Because I want eggs, Brick answers. Four scrambled eggs, served to me by . . .

Molly, the waitress says, giving him a smile. Molly Wald.

. . . by Molly Wald. Any objections to that?

None that I can think of.

So Brick orders his four scrambled eggs, struggling to maintain a light, bantering tone with the skinny, not unfriendly Molly Wald, but underneath it all he's calculating that with prices like these—eggs going at five dollars a pop in a no-account greasy spoon—the money Tobak gave him that morning isn't going to last very long. As Molly turns around and calls out the order into the kitchen behind her, Brick wonders if he should start questioning her about the war or play it closer to the vest and keep his mouth shut. Still undecided, he asks for a cup of coffee.

Sorry, no can do, Molly says, we're all out. Hot tea. I can give you some hot tea if you like.

Okay, Brick says. A pot of tea. After a moment's hesitation, he plucks up his courage and asks: Just out of curiosity, how much is it?

Five bucks.

Five bucks? It seems that everything in here costs five bucks.

Clearly thrown by his comment, Molly leans forward, plants her arms on the counter, and shakes her head. You're kind of dumb, aren't you?

Probably, Brick says.

We stopped using singles and coins six months ago. Where have you been, pal? Are you a foreigner or something?

I don't know. I'm from New York. Does that make me a foreigner or not?

New York City?

Queens.

Molly lets out a sharp little laugh, which seems to convey both contempt and pity for her know-nothing customer. That's rich, she says, really rich. A guy from New York who can't tell his ass from his elbow.

I . . . uh . . . , Brick stammers, I've been sick. Out of commission. You know, in a hospital, and I haven't kept up with what's been going on.

Well, for your information, Mr. Stupid, Molly says, we're in a war, and New York started it.

Oh?

Yes, *oh*. Secession. Maybe you've heard of it. When a state declares independence from the rest of the country. There are sixteen of us now, and God knows when it will end. I'm not saying it's a bad thing, but enough is enough. It wears you out, and pretty soon you're just sick of the whole business.

There was a lot of gunfire last night, Brick says, finally daring to ask a direct question. Who won?

The Federals attacked, but our troops fought them off. I doubt they'll try that again anytime soon.

Which means that things are going to be fairly quiet in Wellington.

At least for now, yeah. Or so they say. But who knows?

A voice from the kitchen announces: *Four scrambled,* and a moment later a white plate appears on the shelf behind Molly. She pivots, takes hold of Brick's meal, and sets it down in front of him. Then she begins preparing the tea.

The eggs prove to be dry and overcooked, and not even some healthy doses of salt and pepper can draw much flavor from them. Half-starved after his twelve-mile walk, Brick shovels one forkful of food into his mouth after another, chewing diligently on the rubbery eggs and washing them down with frequent sips of tea—which isn't hot as advertised, but tepid. No matter, he says to himself. With so many unanswered questions to be dealt with, the quality of the food is the least of his worries. Pausing for a moment about midway through his combat with the eggs, Brick looks over at Molly, who is still standing behind the counter, watching him eat with her arms folded across her chest, shifting the weight of her body now onto her left leg, now onto her right, her green eyes flickering with what appears to be a kind of suppressed mirth.

What's so funny? he asks.

Nothing, she says, shrugging her shoulders. It's just that you're eating so fast, you remind me of a dog we used to have when I was a kid.

Sorry, Brick says. I'm hungry.

So I gathered.

You also might have gathered that I'm new around here, he says. I don't know a soul in Wellington, and I need a place to stay. I was wondering if you had any ideas.

For how long?

I don't know. Maybe a night, maybe a week, maybe forever. It's too soon to tell.

You're pretty vague about it, aren't you?

It can't be helped. I'm in a situation, you see, an odd situation, and I'm kind of stumbling around in the dark. The fact is, I don't even know what day it is.

Thursday, April nineteenth.

April nineteenth. Good. That's just what I would have said. But what year?

Are you kidding?

No, unfortunately not. What year is it?

Two thousand and seven.

Strange.

Why strange?

Because it's the right year, but everything else is wrong. Listen to me, Molly . . .

I'm listening, friend. I'm all ears.

Good. Now, if I said the words *September eleventh* to you, would they have any special meaning?

Not particularly.

And *the World Trade Center*?

The twin towers? Those tall buildings in New York?

Exactly.

What about them?

They're still standing?

Of course they are. What's wrong with you?

Nothing, Brick says, muttering to himself in a barely audible voice. Then, looking down at his half-eaten eggs, he whispers: One nightmare replaces another.

What? I didn't hear you.

Lifting his head and looking Molly straight in the eyes, Brick asks her a final question: And there's no war in Iraq, is there?

If you already know the answer, why ask me?

I just had to be sure. Forgive me.

Look, mister—

Owen. Owen Brick.

All right, Owen. I don't know what your problem is, and I don't know what happened to you in that hospital, but if I were you, I'd finish those eggs before they get cold. I'm going back into the kitchen to make a call. One of my cousins is the night manager of a little hotel around the corner. There could be a vacancy.

Why are you being so nice? You don't even know me.

I'm not being nice. My cousin and I have a deal. Whenever I bring him a new customer, he gives me a ten percent cut on the first night. It's strictly business, spaceman. If he has a room for you, you don't owe me a thing.

It turns out that he does. By the time Brick has swallowed the last of his food (with the aid of yet another gulp of the now-cold tea), Molly has come back from the kitchen to give him the good news. There are three rooms available, she says, two of them for three hundred a night and the third for two hundred. Not knowing how much he can afford, she's taken it upon herself to book him the room for two hundred, a clear indication, Brick thankfully notes, that despite her tough talk about *strictly business*, Molly has reduced her finder's fee by ten dollars as a favor to him. Not such a bad girl, he thinks, no matter how hard she works at hiding it. Brick is feeling so lonely, so discombobulated by the events of the past twenty hours, he wishes she would abandon her post behind the counter and accompany him to the hotel, but he knows she can't, and he's too timid to ask her to make an exception for him. Instead, Molly sketches a diagram on a paper napkin, indicating the route he should follow to reach the Exeter Hotel, which is only one block away. Then he settles the tab, insisting that she accept a ten-dollar tip, and shakes her hand good-bye.

I hope I see you again, he says, suddenly and moronically on the verge of tears.

I'm always around, she replies. From eight to six, Monday through Friday. If you ever want another lousy meal, you know where to come.

The Exeter Hotel is a six-story limestone building in the middle of a block of discount shoe stores and dimly lit bars. It might have been an attractive place sixty or seventy years ago, but one look at the lobby, with its sagging, moth-eaten velvet chairs and dead potted palms, and Brick understands that two hundred dollars doesn't buy you much in Wellington. He's a bit stunned when the clerk behind the front desk insists that he pay for the night in advance, but since he's unfamiliar with local customs, he doesn't bother to protest. The clerk, who could pass for Serge Tobak's twin brother, counts out the four fifty-dollar bills, sweeps them into a drawer below the cracked marble counter, and hands Brick the key to room 406. No signature or proof of identity required. When Brick asks where he can find the elevator, the clerk informs him that it's broken.

Somewhat winded after climbing the four flights of stairs, Brick unlocks the door and enters his room. He observes that the bed has been made, that the white walls look and smell as if they've been freshly painted, that everything is relatively clean, but once he begins to look around in earnest, he is gripped by a pulverizing sense of dread. The room is so bleak and unwelcoming, he imagines that dozens of desperate people have checked into this place over the years with no other purpose than to commit suicide. Where has this impression come from? Is it his own state of mind, he wonders, or can it be borne out by the facts? The sparseness of the furniture, for example: just one bed and one battered wardrobe stranded in an overly large space. No chair, no phone. The absence of any pictures on the walls. The blank, cheerless bathroom, with a

single miniature bar of soap lying in its wrapper on the white
sink, a single white hand towel hanging on the rack, the rusted
enamel in the white tub. Pacing around in an ever-spiraling
funk, Brick decides to turn on the old black-and-white television next to the window. Maybe that will calm him down, he
thinks, or, if luck is with him, maybe a newscast will be on and
he can learn something about the war. A hollow, echoing ping
emerges from the box as he pushes the button. A promising
sign, he says to himself, but then, after a long wait as the machine slowly warms up, no image appears on the screen. Nothing but snow, and the strident hiss of static. He changes the
channel. More snow, more static. He goes around the dial, but
each stop produces the same result. Rather than simply turn
off the television, Brick yanks the cord out of the wall. Then he
sits down on the ancient bed, which groans under the weight of
his body.

Before he has a chance to slump into a miasma of useless
self-pity, someone knocks on the door. No doubt an employee
of the hotel, Brick thinks, but secretly he's hoping it's Molly
Wald, that somehow or other she's managed to dash out of the
diner for a couple of minutes to check on him and make sure
he's all right. Not very probable, of course, and no sooner does
he unlock the door than his fleeting hope is crushed. His visi-
tor isn't Molly, but neither is it an employee of the hotel. Instead, he finds himself standing in front of a tall, attractive
woman with dark hair and blue eyes dressed in black jeans
and a brown leather jacket—clothes similar to the ones Sarge
Serge gave him that morning. As Brick studies her face, he is

convinced they have met before, but his mind refuses to conjure up a memory of where or when.

Hi there, Owen, the woman says, flashing him a bright, brittle smile, and as he looks at her mouth, he notices that she's wearing an intense shade of red lipstick.

I know you, don't I? Brick answers. At least I think I do. Or maybe you just remind me of someone.

Virginia Blaine, the woman announces cheerfully, triumph ringing in her voice. Don't you remember? You had a crush on me in the tenth grade.

Good God, Brick mutters, more lost than ever now. Virginia Blaine. We sat next to each other in Miss Blunt's geometry class.

Aren't you going to let me in?

Of course, of course, he says, stepping out of the doorway and watching her stride across the threshold.

Once she has cast her eyes around the grim, barren room, Virginia turns to him and says: What a horrible place. Why on earth did you check in here?

It's a long story, Brick replies, not wanting to go into it.

This won't do, Owen. We'll have to find you something better.

Maybe tomorrow. I've already paid up for tonight, and I doubt they'd give me my money back now.

There isn't even a chair to sit in.

I realize that. You can sit on the bed if you want to.

Thanks, Virginia says, glancing over at the worn-out green bedspread, I think I'll stand.

What are you doing here? Brick asks, abruptly changing the subject.

I saw you walk into the hotel, and I came up to—

No, no, I don't mean that, he says, cutting her off in mid-sentence. I'm talking about *here,* in Wellington, a city I've never even heard of. In this country, which is supposed to be America but isn't America, at least not the America I know.

I can't tell you. Not yet, anyway.

I go to bed with my wife in New York. We make love, we fall asleep, and when I wake up I'm lying in a hole in the middle of goddamned nowhere, dressed in a fucking army uniform. What the hell is going on?

Calm down, Owen. I know it's a bit disorienting at first, but you'll get used to it, I promise.

I don't want to get used to it. I want to go back to my life.

You will. And a lot sooner than you think.

Well, at least that's something, Brick says, not sure whether he should believe her or not. But if I'm able to go back, what about you?

I don't want to go back. I've been here a long time now, and I like it better than where I used to be.

A long time. . . . So when you stopped coming to school, it wasn't because you and your parents had moved away.

No.

I missed you a lot. For about three months, I'd been screwing up my courage to ask you out on a date, and then, just when I was ready to do it, you were gone.

It couldn't be helped. I didn't have any choice.

What keeps you here? Are you married? Do you have any kids?

No kids, but I used to be married. My husband was killed at the beginning of the war.

I'm sorry.

I'm sorry, too. And I'm also a little sorry to hear that you're married. I haven't forgotten you, Owen. I know it was a long time ago, but I wanted to go out on that date just as much as you did.

Now you tell me.

It's the truth. I mean, whose idea do you think it was to bring you here?

You're joking. Come on, Virginia, why would you do something that awful to me?

I wanted to see you again. And I also thought you'd be the perfect man for the job.

What job?

Don't be coy, Owen. You know what I'm talking about.

Tobak. The clown who calls himself Sarge Serge.

And Lou Frisk. You were supposed to go to him straightaway, remember?

I was tired. I'd been walking all day on an empty stomach, and I needed to eat something and take a nap. I was about to climb into bed when you knocked on the door.

Bad luck. We're working on a tight schedule, and we have to go to Frisk now.

I can't. I'm just too exhausted. Let me sleep for a couple of hours, and then I'll go with you.

I really shouldn't . . .

Please, Virginia. For old times' sake.

All right, she says, looking down at her wristwatch. I'll give you an hour. It's four-thirty now. Expect a knock on your door at five-thirty sharp.

Thank you.

But no funny business, Owen. Okay?

Of course not.

After giving him a warm, affectionate smile, Virginia opens her arms and hugs Brick good-bye. It's so good to see you again, she whispers into his ear. Brick remains mute, his arms at his sides, a hundred thoughts darting through his head. Finally, Virginia lets go of him, pats him on the cheek, and makes her way to the door, which she opens with a quick, downward thrust on the handle. Before letting herself out, she turns and says: Five-thirty.

Five-thirty, Brick echoes, and then the door bangs shut, and Virginia Blaine is gone.

Brick already has a plan—and a set of principles. Under no circumstances does he want to meet Frisk or carry out the job they've assigned him. He is not going to murder anyone, he will not do anyone's bidding, he will keep himself out of sight for as long as necessary. Since Virginia knows where he is, he will have to leave the hotel at once and never return. Where to go next is the most immediate problem, and he can think of only three possible solutions. Return to the diner and ask Molly Wald for help. If she isn't willing to give it, then what? Roam the streets and look for another hotel, or else wait for nightfall and then slip out of Wellington.

He gives himself ten minutes, more than enough time for Virginia to get down the four flights of stairs and leave the Exeter. She could be waiting in the lobby, of course, or keeping watch on the hotel entrance from across the street, but if she isn't in the lobby, he will make his exit through a back door, assuming there is a back door and he can find it. And what if she happens to be in the lobby, after all? He will make a run for it, pure and simple. Brick might not be the fastest man in the world, but during his conversation with Virginia he noticed that she was wearing high-heeled boots, and surely a man in flat shoes can outrun a woman in high-heeled boots any day of the week.

As for the hug and the affectionate smile, as for professing to want to see him again and her regret at not having gone out with him in high school, Brick is nothing if not skeptical. Virginia Blaine, the heartthrob of his fifteen-year-old self, was the prettiest girl in the class, and every boy swooned with lust and silent longing whenever she walked by. He wasn't telling the truth when he said he was about to ask her out on a date. There was no question that he wanted to ask, but at that point in his life, he never would have dared.

Leather jacket zipped, backpack slung over his right shoulder, down Brick goes, taking the rear stairwell, the fire exit, which mercifully allows him to bypass the lobby altogether and leads to a metal door that opens onto a street parallel to the front entrance of the hotel. No sign of Virginia anywhere, and so heartened is our frazzled hero by his successful escape, he feels a momentary surge of optimism, sensing that he can finally add the word *hope* to the lexicon of his miseries. He walks along quickly, sliding past knots of pedestrians, dodging a boy on a pogo stick, slackening his pace briefly at the approach of four soldiers carrying rifles, listening to the ever-present clank of bicycles rolling down the street. A turn, another turn, and then one more, and there he is, standing in front of the Pulaski Diner, the restaurant where Molly works.

Brick goes in, and once again the place is empty. Now that he understands the circumstances, this hardly comes as a surprise to him, since why would anyone bother to go to a restaurant that has no food? Not a customer to be seen, therefore, but more distressing is the absence of Molly as well. Wondering if she hasn't gone home early, Brick calls out her name, and when she fails to appear, he calls it out again. After several anxious seconds, he is relieved to see her walk into the room, but once she recognizes him, the boredom in her face instantly turns to worry, perhaps even anger.

Is everything okay? she asks, her voice sounding tight and defensive.

Yes and no, Brick says.

What does that mean? Did they give you any trouble at the hotel?

No trouble. They were expecting me. I paid for one night in advance and went upstairs.

What about the room? Any problem with that?

Let me tell you, Molly, Brick says, unable to suppress the

smile that is spreading across his lips, I've traveled all over the world, and when it comes to first-class accommodations, I mean top-of-the-line comfort and elegance, nothing comes close to room four-oh-six at the Exeter Hotel in Wellington.

Molly smiles broadly at his facetious remark, and all at once she looks like a different person. Yeah, I know, she says. It's a classy place, isn't it?

Seeing that smile, Brick suddenly understands the cause of her alarm. Her initial assumption was that he marched back here to complain, to accuse her of having swindled him, but now that she knows otherwise, she has let down her guard, relaxed into a more amiable attitude.

It has nothing to do with the hotel, he says. It's about that situation I mentioned to you before. A bunch of people are after me. They want me to do something I don't want to do, and now they know I'm staying at the Exeter. Which means I can't stay there anymore. That's why I came back. To ask for your help.

Why me?

Because you're the only person I know.

You don't know me, Molly says, shifting the weight of her body from her right leg to her left. I served you some eggs, I found a room for you, we talked for about five minutes. I hardly call that knowing me.

You're right. I don't know you. But I couldn't think of anywhere else to go.

Why should I stick my neck out for you? You're probably in some kind of trouble. Police trouble or army trouble. Or maybe you escaped from that hospital. The loony bin would be my guess. Give me one good reason why I should help you.

I can't. Not a single one, Brick says, dismayed at how badly he misjudged this girl, how foolish he was to think he could count on her. The only thing I can offer you is money, he adds, remembering the envelope of fifties in the backpack. If you know of a place where I could hide out for a while, I'll be glad to pay you.

Ah, well, that's different, isn't it? says the transparent, not-so-cunning Molly. How much money are we talking about?

I don't know. You tell me.

I suppose I could put you up in my apartment for a night or two. The sofa's long enough to hold that body of yours, I think. But no hanky-panky. My boyfriend lives with me, and he has a bad temper, if you know what I mean, so don't get any dumb ideas.

I'm married. I don't go in for stuff like that.

That's a good one. There isn't a married man in this world who'd pass up some extra nooky if it came his way.

Maybe I don't live in this world.

Yeah, maybe you don't at that. That would explain a lot of things, wouldn't it?

So, how much are you going to charge? Brick asks, eager to complete the transaction.

Two hundred bucks.

Two hundred? That's pretty steep, don't you think?

You don't know crap, mister. Around here, that's rock bottom, as low as it gets. Take it or leave it.

All right, Brick says, bowing his head and letting out a long, mournful sigh. I'll take it.

Suddenly, an urgent need to empty my bladder. I shouldn't have drunk that last glass of wine, but the temptation was too strong, and the fact is I like going to bed a little tipsy. The apple juice bottle is sitting on the floor next to the bed, but as I reach out and grope for it in the dark, I can't seem to find it. The bottle was Miriam's idea—to spare me the pain and difficulty of having to get out of bed and hobble off to the bathroom in the middle of the night. An excellent idea, but the whole point is to have the bottle close at hand, and on this particular night my waving, extended fingers make no contact with the glass. The only solution is to turn on the bedside lamp, but once that happens, any chance I have of falling asleep will be gone for good. The bulb is just fifteen watts, but in the ink-black dark of this room, switching it on will be like exposing myself to a searing blast of fire. I'll go blind for a few seconds, and then, as my pupils gradually expand, I'll be wide awake, and even after I turn off the lamp, my brain will go on churning until dawn. I know this from long experience, a lifetime of battling against myself in the trenches of night. Oh well, nothing to be done, not one bloody thing. I switch on. I go blind. I blink slowly as my eyes adjust, and then I catch sight of the bottle, standing on the floor a mere two inches from its usual spot. I lean over, extend my body a little farther, and take hold of the damn thing. Then, throwing back the covers, I inch myself into a sitting position—carefully, carefully, so as not to rouse the ire of my shattered leg—twist off the top of the bottle, stick my pecker into the hole, and let the pee come pouring out. It never fails to satisfy, that moment when the gush begins, and then watching the bubbling yellow liquid cascade into the bottle as the glass grows warm in my hand. How many times does a person urinate over the course of seventy-two years? I could do the calculations, but why bother now that the job is nearly done? As I remove my penis from the hole, I look down at my old comrade and wonder if I'll ever have sex again, if I'll ever run across another woman who will want to go to bed with me and spend a night in my arms. I push down the thought, tell myself to desist, for therein lies the way to madness. Why did you have to die, Sonia? Why couldn't I have gone first?

I recap the bottle, return it to its proper place on the floor, and pull the blankets over me. What now? To turn off the light or not to turn off the light? I want to go back to my story and discover what happens to Owen Brick, but the latest installments of Miriam's book are lying on the lower shelf of the bedside table, and I promised to read them and give her my comments. After all the movie watching with Katya, I've fallen behind, and it irks me to think I've let her down. Just for a while, then, another chapter or two—for Miriam's sake.

Rose Hawthorne, the youngest of Nathaniel Hawthorne's three children, born in 1851, just thirteen when her father died, redheaded Rose, known to the family as Rosebud, a woman who lived two lives, the first one sad, tormented, failed, the second one remarkable. I've often asked myself why

Miriam chose to take on this project, but I think I'm beginning to understand now. Her last book was a life of John
Donne, the crown prince of poets, the genius of geniuses, and
then she embarks on an investigation of a woman who floun-
dered through the world for forty-five years, a truculent and
difficult person, a confessed "stranger to herself," trying her
hand first at music, then at painting, and after getting nowhere
with either of those pursuits, turning to poetry and short
stories, some of which she managed to publish (no doubt on
the strength of her father's name), but the work was heavy and
awkward, mediocre at best—excluding one line from a poem
quoted in Miriam's manuscript, which I like enormously: *As
the weird world rolls on.*

Add to the public portrait the private facts of her elopement
at twenty with young writer George Lathrop, a man of talent
who never fulfilled his promise, the bitter conflicts of that marriage, the separation, the reconciliation, the death of their only
child at the age of four, the final separation, Rose's protracted
squabbles with her brother and sister, and one begins to think:
why bother, why spend your time exploring the soul of such
an insignificant, unhappy person? But then, in midlife, Rose
underwent a transformation. She became a Catholic, took holy
vows, and founded an order of nuns called the Servants of Relief for Incurable Cancer, devoting her last thirty years to caring
for the terminally ill poor, a passionate defender of every person's right to die with dignity. *The weird world rolls on.* In other
words, as with Donne, Rose Hawthorne's life was a story of
conversion, and that must have been the attraction, the thing

that sparked Miriam's interest in her. Why that should interest her is another question, but I believe it comes directly from her mother: a fundamental conviction that people have the power to change. That was Sonia's influence, not mine, and Miriam is probably a better person for it, but brilliant as my daughter is, there's also something naïve and fragile about her, and I wish to God she would learn that the rotten acts human beings commit against one another are not just aberrations—they're an essential part of who we are. She would suffer less that way. The world wouldn't collapse every time something bad happened to her, and she wouldn't be crying herself to sleep every other night.

I'm not going to pretend that divorce isn't a cruel business. Unspeakable suffering, crippling despair, demonic rage, and the constant cloud of sorrow in the head, which gradually turns into a kind of mourning, as if one were grieving a death. But Richard walked out on Miriam five years ago, and you'd think by now that she would have adjusted to her new circumstances, put herself back in circulation, attempted to reconfigure her life. But all her energy has gone into her teaching and writing, and whenever I bring up the subject of other men, she bristles. Luckily, Katya was already eighteen and off at college when the breakup happened, and she was old enough and strong enough to absorb the shock without going to pieces. Miriam had a much harder time of it when Sonia and I split up. She was just fifteen, a far more vulnerable age, and even though Sonia and I got back together nine years later, the damage had already been done. It's hard enough for grown-ups to live through a divorce, but it's worse for the kids. They're entirely powerless, and they bear the brunt of the pain.

Miriam and Richard made the same mistake that Sonia and I did: they married too young. In our case, we were both twenty-two—not such an uncommon occurrence back in 1957. But when Miriam and Richard walked down the aisle a quarter of a century later, she was the same age her mother had been. Richard was a little older, twenty-four or twenty-five, I think, but the world had changed by then, and they were little more than babies, two crackerjack baby students doing postgraduate work at Yale, and within a couple of years they had a baby of their own. Didn't Miriam understand that Richard might eventually grow restless? Didn't she realize that a forty-year-old professor standing in front of a room of female undergraduates could become entranced by those young bodies? It's the oldest story in the world, but the hardworking, loyal, high-strung Miriam wasn't paying attention. Not even with her own mother's story burned deeply in her mind—that awful moment when her wretch of a father, after eighteen years of marriage, ran off with a woman of twenty-six. I was forty then. Beware of men in their forties.

Why am I doing this? Why do I persist in traveling down these old, tired paths; why this compulsion to pick at old wounds and make myself bleed again? It would be impossible to exaggerate the contempt I sometimes feel for myself. I was supposed to be looking at Miriam's manuscript, but here I am

staring at a crack in the wall and dredging up remnants from
the past, broken things that can never be repaired. Give me
my story. That's all I want now—my little story to keep the
ghosts away. Before switching off the lamp, I turn at random to
another page in the manuscript and fall upon this: the final two
paragraphs of Rose's memoir of her father, written in 1896, de-
scribing the last time she ever saw him.

*It seemed to me a terrible thing that one so peculiarly strong,
sentient, luminous as my father should grow feebler and fainter,
and finally ghostly still and white. Yet when his step was totter-
ing and his frame that of a wraith, he was as dignified as in the
days of greater pride, holding himself, in military self-
command, even more erect than before. He did not omit to come
in his very best black coat to the dinner-table, where the extremely prosaic fare had no effect on the distinction of the meal.
He hated failure, dependence, and disorder, broken rules and
weariness of discipline, as he hated cowardice. I cannot express
how brave he seemed to me. The last time I saw him, he was
leaving the house to take the journey for his health which led
suddenly to the next world. My mother was to go to the station
with him—she who, at the moment when it was said that he
died, staggered and groaned, though so far from him, telling us
that something seemed to be sapping all her strength; I could
hardly bear to let my eyes rest upon her shrunken, suffering form
on this day of farewell. My father certainly knew, what she
vaguely felt, that he would never return.*

*Like a snow image of an unbending but old, old man, he
stood for a moment gazing at me. My mother sobbed as she*

walked beside him to the carriage. We have missed him in the
sunshine, in the storm, in the twilight, ever since.

I switch off, and once again I'm in the dark, engulfed by the
endless, soothing dark. Somewhere in the distance, I hear the
sounds of a truck driving down an empty country road. I listen
to the air rushing in and out of my nostrils. According to the
clock on the bedside table, which I checked before turning off
the lamp, the time is twenty past twelve. Hours and hours until daybreak, the bulk of the night still in front of me. . . .
Hawthorne didn't care. If the South wanted to secede from the
country, he said, let them go and good riddance. The weird
world, the battered world, the weird world rolling on as wars
flame all around us: the chopped-off arms in Africa, the
chopped-off heads in Iraq, and in my own head this other war,
an imaginary war on home ground, America cracking apart,
the noble experiment finally dead. My thoughts drift back to
Wellington, and suddenly I can see Owen Brick again, sitting
in one of the booths at the Pulaski Diner, watching Molly
Wald wipe down the tables and counter as six o'clock approaches. Then they're outdoors, walking together in silence
as she leads him toward her place, the sidewalks clogged with
exhausted-looking men and women shuffling home from work,
soldiers with rifles standing guard at the main intersections, a
pinkish sky gloaming overhead. Brick has lost all confidence
in Molly. Realizing that she can't be trusted, that no one can
be trusted, he ducked into the men's room at the diner about

twenty minutes before they left and transferred the envelope of fifty-dollar bills from the backpack to the right front pocket of his jeans. A smaller chance of being robbed that way, he felt, and when he goes to bed that night, he has every intention of keeping his pants on. In the men's room, he finally took the trouble to examine the money and was encouraged to see the face of Ulysses S. Grant engraved on the front of each bill. That proved to him that this America, this other America, which hasn't lived through September 11 or the war in Iraq, nevertheless has strong historical links to the America he knows. The question is: at what point did the two stories begin to diverge?

Molly, Brick says, breaking the silence ten minutes into their walk, do you mind if I ask you something?

It depends on what it is, she answers.

Have you ever heard of the Second World War?

The waitress lets out a short, ill-tempered grunt. What do you think I am? she says. A retard? Of course I've heard of it.

And what about Vietnam?

My grandfather was one of the first soldiers they shipped out.

If I said *the New York Yankees,* what would you say?

Come on, everybody knows that.

What would you say? Brick repeats.

With an exasperated sigh, Molly turns to him and announces in a sardonic voice: The New York Yankees? They're those girls who dance at Radio City Music Hall.

Very good. And the Rockettes are a baseball team, right?

Exactly.

Okay. One last question, and then I'll stop.

You're a real pain in the ass, you know that?

Sorry. I know you think I'm stupid, but it isn't my fault.

No, I guess not. You just happened to be born that way.

Who's the president?

President? What are you talking about? We don't have a president.

No? Then who's in charge of the government?

The prime minister, birdbrain. Jesus Christ, what planet do you come from?

I see. The independent states have a prime minister. But what about the Federals? Do they still have a president?

Of course.

What's his name?

Bush.

George W.?

That's right. George W. Bush.

Sticking to his word, Brick refrains from asking any more questions, and once again the two of them walk through the streets in silence. A couple of minutes later, Molly points to a four-story wood-frame building on a low-rent residential block lined with similar four-story wooden buildings, all of them in need of a paint job. 628 Cumberland Avenue. Here we are, she says, extracting a key from her purse and unlocking the front door, and then Brick follows her up two flights of wobbly stairs to the apartment she occupies with her unnamed boyfriend. It's a small but tidy flat, consisting of one bedroom, a living room, a kitchen, and a bathroom with a shower but no tub.

Looking around the place, Brick is struck by the fact that there's no television or radio either. When he remarks on this to Molly, she tells him that all the transmission towers in the state were blown up in the first weeks of the war, and the government doesn't have enough money to rebuild them.

Maybe after the war is over, Brick says.

Yeah, maybe, Molly answers, sitting down on the living room sofa and lighting up a cigarette. But the thing is, nobody seems to care anymore. It was hard at first—*my God, no TV!*—but then you kind of get used to it, and after another year or two, you begin to like it. The stillness, I mean. No more voices shouting at you twenty-four hours a day. It's an old-fashioned sort of life now, I guess, the way things must have been a hundred years ago. You want news, you read the paper. You want to see a movie, you go to the theater. No more couch potatoes. I know a lot of people have died, and I know things are really tough out there, but maybe it's all been worth it. *Maybe.* Just maybe. If the war doesn't end soon, everything will turn to shit.

Brick is at a loss to explain it, but he realizes that Molly is no longer talking to him as if he were a dunce. How to account for this unexpected shift in tone? The fact that her job is done for the day and she's sitting comfortably in her apartment puffing on a cigarette? The fact that she's begun to feel sorry for him? Or, conversely, the fact that he's made her two hundred dollars richer and she's decided to stop poking fun at him? In any case, Brick thinks, a girl of many moods, perhaps not as crass as she seems to be, but not so terribly bright either.

There are a hundred more questions he would like to ask her, but he decides not to push his luck.

Stubbing out her cigarette, Molly stands up and tells Brick that she's meeting her boyfriend for dinner across town in less than an hour. She walks over to a closet between the bedroom and the kitchen, pulls out two sheets, two blankets, and a pillow, then carries them into the living room and plops them down on the sofa.

There you are, she says. Bedding for your bed, which isn't a real bed. I hope it's not too lumpy.

I'm so tired, Brick answers, I could sleep on a pile of rocks.

If you get hungry, there's some stuff to eat in the kitchen. A can of soup, a loaf of bread, some sliced turkey. You can make yourself a sandwich.

How much?

What do you mean?

How much will it cost me?

Cut it out. I'm not going to charge you for a little food. You've already paid me enough.

And what about breakfast tomorrow morning?

Fine by me. We don't have a lot, though. Just coffee and toast.

Without waiting for Brick to answer, Molly rushes off to the bedroom to change her clothes. The door slams shut, and Brick begins making the bed that isn't a bed. When he's finished, he walks around the room looking for newspapers and magazines, hoping to find something that will tell him about the war, something that will give him a clue about where he is,

some scrap of information that will help him understand a little more about the bewildering country he's landed in. But
there are no magazines or newspapers in the living room—
only a small bookcase crammed with paperback mysteries and
thrillers, which he has no desire to read.

He returns to the sofa, sits down, leans his head against the
upholstered backrest, and promptly dozes off.

When he opens his eyes thirty minutes later, the bedroom
door is ajar, and Molly is gone.

He searches the bedroom for newspapers and magazines—
with no success.

Then he walks into the kitchen to heat up a can of vegetable
soup and fix himself a turkey sandwich. He notes that the
brands are familiar to him: Progresso, Boar's Head, Arnold's.
Washing the dishes after eating this *prosaic fare*, he looks at the
white telephone attached to the wall and wonders what would
happen if he tried to call Flora.

He takes the receiver off the hook, dials the number of his
apartment in Jackson Heights, and quickly learns the answer.
The number is out of service.

He dries the dishes and puts them back in the cupboard.
Then, after turning off the kitchen light, he walks into the living room and thinks about Flora, his dark-haired Argentinian
bedmate, his little spitfire, his wife of the past three years.
What she must be going through, he says to himself.

He turns off the lights in the living room. He undoes the
laces of his shoes. He crawls under the covers. He falls asleep.

Some hours later, he is woken by the sound of a key entering

the lock of the apartment door. Keeping his eyes shut, Brick listens to the scraping of footsteps, the low-pitched rumble of a male voice, the sharper, more metallic voice of his female companion, no doubt Molly, yes, indeed Molly, who addresses the man as Duke, and then a light goes on, which registers as a crimson glare undulating on the surface of his eyelids. They both sound a bit drunk, and as the light goes off and they clomp into the bedroom—where another light immediately goes on—Brick gathers that they're quarreling about something. Before the door shuts, he catches the words *don't like it, two hundred, risky, harmless,* and understands that he is the subject of the argument and that Duke is none too happy about his presence in the house.

Managing to fall asleep again after the ruckus in the bedroom dies down (sounds of copulation: a grunting Duke, a yelping Molly, squeaking mattress and springs), Brick then floats off into a complex dream about Flora. At first, he's talking to her on the telephone. It isn't Flora's voice, however, with its thick, rolling *r*'s and singsong lilt, but the voice of Virginia Blaine, and Virginia/Flora is begging him to fly—not walk, but fly—to a certain corner in Buffalo, New York, where she'll be standing naked under a transparent raincoat, holding a red umbrella in one hand and a white tulip in the other. Brick begins to weep, telling her that he doesn't know how to fly, at which point Virginia/Flora shouts angrily into the phone that she never wants to see him again and hangs up. Stunned by her vehemence, Brick shakes his head and mutters to himself: But I'm not in Buffalo today, I'm in Worcester, Massachusetts.

Then he's walking down a street in Jackson Heights, dressed in his Great Zavello costume with the long black cape, looking for his apartment building. But the building is gone, and in its place there is a one-story wooden cottage with a sign above the door that reads: ALL-AMERICAN DENTAL CLINIC. He walks in, and there's Flora, the real Flora, dressed in a white nurse's uniform. I'm so glad you could come, Mr. Brick, she says, apparently not recognizing him, and then she's leading him into an office and gesturing for him to sit down in a dental chair. It's such a shame, she says, picking up a pair of large, gleaming pliers, it's such a shame, but it looks like we're going to have to pull out all your teeth. All of them? Brick asks, suddenly terrified. Yes, Flora answers, all of them. But don't worry. After we're done, the doctor will give you a new face.

The dream stops there. Someone is shaking Brick's shoulder and barking words at him in a loud voice, and as the groggy dreamer at last opens his eyes, he sees a large man with broad shoulders and muscular arms towering above him. One of those bodybuilder types, Brick thinks, Duke the boyfriend, the guy with the bad temper, dressed in a tight-fitting black T-shirt and blue boxer shorts, telling him to get the fuck out of the apartment.

I paid good money— Brick begins.

For one night, Duke shouts. The night's up now, and out you go.

Just a minute, just a minute, Brick says, raising his right hand as a sign of his peaceful intentions. Molly promised me

breakfast. Coffee and toast. Just let me have some coffee, and then I'll be on my way.

No coffee. No toast. No nothing.

What if I paid you for it? A little extra, I mean.

Don't you understand English?

And with those words, Duke bends down, grabs hold of Brick's sweater, and yanks him to his feet. Now that he's standing, Brick has a clear view of the bedroom door, and the moment he catches sight of it, out comes Molly, securing the sash of her bathrobe and then running her hands through her hair.

Stop it, she says to Duke. You don't have to play rough.

Pipe down, he answers. You made this mess, and now I'm cleaning it up.

Molly shrugs, then looks at Brick with a small, apologetic smile. Sorry, she says. I guess you'd better be going now.

Slipping his feet into his shoes without bothering to tie the laces, then retrieving his leather jacket from the foot of the sofa and putting it on, Brick says to her: I don't get it. I give you all that money, and now you throw me out. It doesn't make sense.

Rather than answer him, Molly looks down at the floor and shrugs again. That apathetic gesture carries all the force of a defection, a betrayal. With no ally to stand up for him, Brick decides to leave without further protest. He bends down and picks up the green backpack from the floor, but no sooner does he turn to go than Duke snatches it out of his hands.

What's this? he asks.

My stuff, Brick says. Obviously.

Your stuff? Duke replies. I don't think so, funny man.

What are you talking about?

It's mine now.

Yours? You can't do that. Everything I own is in there.

Then try and get it back.

Brick understands that Duke is itching for a fight—and that the bag is merely a pretext. He also knows that if he tangles with Molly's boyfriend, there is every chance he will be ripped apart. Or so his mind tells him the instant he hears Duke issue his challenge, but Brick is no longer thinking with his mind, for the outrage surging through him has overwhelmed all reason, and if he allows this bully to get his way without offering some form of resistance, he will lose whatever respect he still has for himself. So Brick takes his stand, unexpectedly wrenching the bag out of Duke's grasp, and immediately after that the drubbing begins, an assault so one-sided and short-lived that the big man floors Brick with just three blows: a left to the gut, a right to the face, and a knee to the balls. Pain floods into every corner of the magician's body, and as he rolls around on the tattered rug gasping for breath, one hand clutching his stomach and the other clamped over his scrotum, he sees blood dripping from the wound that has opened on his cheek, and then, lying in the gathering puddle of red, a fragment of a tooth—the lower half of one of his left incisors. He is only dimly aware of Molly's screams, which sound as if they are coming from ten blocks away. A moment after that, he is aware of nothing.

When he picks up the thread of his own story, Brick finds himself on his feet, maneuvering his body down the stairs as he clings to the banister with both hands, slowly descending to the ground floor, a single step at a time. The backpack is gone, which means that the gun and the bullets are also gone, not to speak of everything else that was in the bag, but as Brick pauses to reach into the right front pocket of his jeans, the trace of a smile flits across his bruised mouth—the bitter smile of the not quite vanquished. The money is still there. No longer the thousand that Tobak gave him the previous morning, but five hundred and sixty-five dollars is better than nothing, he thinks, more than enough to get him a room somewhere and a bite to eat. That's as far as his thoughts can take him now. To hide, to wash the blood off his face, to fill his stomach if and when his appetite returns.

However modest these plans might be, they are thwarted the moment he leaves the building and steps onto the sidewalk. Directly in front of him, standing with her arms folded and her back resting against the door of a military jeep, Virginia Blaine is eyeing Brick with a disgusted look on her face.

No monkey business, she says. You promised me.

Virginia, Brick replies, doing his best to play dumb, what are you doing here?

Ignoring his remark, the former queen of Miss Blunt's geometry class shakes her head and snaps back: We were supposed to meet at five-thirty yesterday afternoon. You stood me up.

Something happened, and I had to leave at the last minute.

You mean *I* happened, and you ran away.

Unable to think of an answer, Brick says nothing.

You don't look so good, Owen, Virginia continues.

No, I don't suppose I do. I just got the shit kicked out of me.

You should watch the company you keep. That Rothstein's a tough fellow.

Who's Rothstein?

Duke. Molly's boyfriend.

You know him?

He works with us. He's one of our best men.

He's an animal. A sadistic creep.

It was all an act, Owen. To teach you a lesson.

Oh? Brick snorts, indignation rising within him. And what lesson is that? The son of a bitch knocked out one of my teeth.

Just be glad it wasn't all of them.

Very nice, Brick mumbles, with a sarcastic edge to his voice, and then, all of a sudden, the final chapter of the dream comes rushing back to him: the All-American Dental Clinic, Flora and the pliers, the new face. Well, Brick thinks, as he touches the wound on his cheek, I got my new face, didn't I? Thanks to Rothstein's fist.

You can't win, Virginia says. Everywhere you go, someone is watching you. You'll never get away from us.

According to you, Brick says, not yet willing to give in, but knowing in his heart that Virginia is right.

Ergo, my dear Owen, this little interlude of dawdling and hide-and-seek has come to an end. Hop into the jeep. It's time for you to talk to Frisk.

No dice, Virginia. I can't hop, and I can't run, and I can't go anywhere yet. My face is bleeding, my balls are on fire, and every muscle in my stomach is torn to shreds. I have to patch myself up first. Then I'll talk to your man. But at least let me take a goddamn bath.

For the first time since the conversation began, Virginia smiles. Poor baby, she says, simpering with compassion, but whether this new concern for him is real or false is far from clear to Brick.

Are you with me or not? he asks.

Climb in, she says, patting the door of the jeep. Of course I'm with you. I'll take you back to my house, and we'll fix you up there. It's still early. Lou can wait a little while. As long as you see him before dark, we'll be okay.

With that reassurance, Brick hobbles over to the jeep and hoists his sorry carcass into the passenger seat as Virginia slips in behind the wheel. Once she starts the engine, she launches into a long, meandering account of the civil war, no doubt feeling an obligation to fill him in on the historical background of the conflict, but the problem is that Brick is in no condition to follow what she's saying, and as they lurch along over the potholed streets of Wellington, every jolt and bump sends a fresh attack of pain coursing through his body. To compound the trouble, the noise of the engine is so loud that it nearly swallows up Virginia's voice, and in order to hear anything at all, Brick must strain himself to the limit of his powers, which are diminished at best, if not entirely obliterated. Clutching the bottom of the seat with his two hands, pressing the soles of his shoes onto the floor to brace himself against the next bounce of the chassis, he keeps his eyes shut throughout the twenty-minute drive, and from the ten thousand facts that come tumbling down on him between Molly's apartment and Virginia's house, this is what he manages to retain:

The election of 2000 . . . just after the Supreme Court decision . . . protests . . . riots in the major cities . . . a movement to abolish the Electoral College . . . defeat of the bill in Congress . . . a new movement . . . led by the mayor and borough presidents of New York City . . . secession . . . passed by the state legislature in 2003 . . . Federal troops attack . . . Albany, Buffalo, Syracuse, Rochester . . . New York City bombed, eighty thousand dead . . . but the movement grows . . . in 2004, Maine, New Hampshire, Vermont, Massachusetts, Connecticut, New Jersey, and Pennsylvania join New York in the Independent States of America . . . later that year, California, Oregon, and Washington break off to form their own republic, Pacifica . . . in 2005, Ohio, Michigan, Illinois, Wisconsin, and Minnesota join the Independent States . . . the European Union recognizes the existence of the new country . . . diplomatic relations are established . . . then Mexico . . . then the countries of Central and South America . . . Russia follows, then Japan. . . . Meanwhile, the fighting continues, often horrendous, the toll of casualties steadily mounting . . . U.N. resolutions ignored by the Federals, but until now no nuclear weapons, which would mean death to everyone on both sides. . . . Foreign policy: no meddling anywhere. . . . Domestic policy: universal health insurance, no more oil, no more cars or planes, a fourfold increase in teachers' salaries (to attract the brightest students to the profession), strict gun control, free education and job training for the poor . . . all in the realm of fantasy for the moment, a dream of the future, since the war drags on, and the state of emergency is still in force.

The jeep slows down and gradually comes to a stop. As Virginia turns off the ignition, Brick opens his eyes and discovers that he is no longer in the heart of Wellington. They have come to a wealthy suburban street of large Tudor houses with pristine front lawns, tulip beds, forsythia and rhododendron bushes, the myriad trappings of the good life. As he climbs out of the jeep and looks down the block, however, he notices that several houses are standing in ruins: broken windows, charred walls, gaping holes in the facades, abandoned husks where people once lived. Brick assumes that the neighborhood was shelled during the war, but he doesn't ask any questions about it. Instead, pointing to the house they are about to enter, he blandly remarks: This is quite a place, Virginia. You seem to have done pretty well for yourself.

My husband was a corporate lawyer, she says flatly, in no mood to talk about the past. He made a lot of money.

Virginia opens the door with a key, and they walk into the house . . .

A warm bath, lying in water up to his neck for twenty minutes, thirty minutes, inert, tranquil, alone. After which he puts on the white terry-cloth robe of Virginia's dead husband, walks into the bedroom, and sits down in a chair as Virginia patiently applies an antibacterial astringent to the gash on his cheek and then covers the wound with a small bandage. Brick is beginning to feel somewhat better. The wonders of water, he says to himself, realizing that the pain in his stomach and nether parts has all but vanished. His cheek still smarts, but eventually that discomfort will abate as well. As for the broken tooth, there is nothing to be done until he can visit a dentist and have a cap put on it, but he doubts that will happen anytime soon. For now (as confirmed when he studied his face in the bathroom mirror), the effect is altogether repulsive. A few centimeters of missing enamel and he looks like a broken-down bum, a pea-brained yokel. Fortunately, the gap is visible only when he smiles, and in Brick's present state, the last thing he wants to do is smile. Unless the nightmare ends, he thinks, there's a good chance he'll never smile again for the rest of his life.

Twenty minutes later, now dressed and sitting in the kitchen with Virginia—who has prepared him toast and coffee, the same minimal breakfast that nearly cost him his life earlier that morning—Brick is answering the tenth question she has asked him about Flora. He finds her curiosity puzzling. If she is the person responsible for bringing him to this place, then it would seem likely that she already knows everything about him, including his marriage to Flora. But Virginia is insatiable, and now Brick begins to wonder if all this questioning isn't simply a ploy to hold him in the house, to make him lose track of the time so that he won't try to run off again before Frisk shows up. He wants to run, that's certain, but after the long soak in the tub and the terry-cloth robe and the gentleness of her fingers as she put the bandage on his face, something in him has begun to soften toward Virginia, and he can feel the old flames of his adolescence slowly igniting again.

I met her in Manhattan, he says. About three and a half years ago. A fancy birthday party for a kid on the Upper East Side. I was the magician, and she was one of the caterers.

Is she beautiful, Owen?

To me she is. Not beautiful in the way you are, Virginia, with your incredible face and long body. Flora's little, not even five-four, just a slip of a thing, really, but she has these big burning eyes and all this tangly dark hair and the best laugh I've ever heard.

Do you love her?

Of course.

And she loves you?

Yes. Most of the time, anyway. Flora has a huge temper, and she can fly off into these maniacal tirades. Whenever we fight, I begin to think the only reason she married me was because she wanted her American citizenship. But it doesn't happen very often. Nine days out of ten, we're good together. We really are.

What about babies?

They're on the agenda. We started trying a couple of months ago.

Don't give up. That was my mistake. I waited too long, and now look at me. No husband, no children, nothing.

You're still young. You're still the prettiest girl on the block. Someone else will come along, I'm sure of it.

Before Virginia can answer him, the doorbell rings. She

stands up, muttering *Shit* under her breath as if she means it, as if she honestly resents the intrusion, but Brick knows that he's cornered now, and any chance of escape is gone. Before leaving the kitchen, Virginia turns to him and says: I called while you were taking your bath. I told him to come between four and five, but I guess he couldn't wait. I'm sorry, Owen. I wanted to have those hours with you and charm your pants off. I really did. I wanted to fuck your brains out. Just remember that when you go back.

Back? You mean I'm going back?

Lou will explain. That's his job. I'm just a personnel officer, a little cog in a big machine.

Lou Frisk turns out to be a dour-looking man in his early fifties, somewhat on the short side, with narrow shoulders, wire-rimmed glasses, and the marred skin of someone who once suffered from acne. He's dressed in a green V-neck sweater with a white shirt and plaid tie, and in his left hand he's carrying a black satchel that resembles a doctor's bag. The moment he enters the kitchen, he puts down the bag and says: You've been avoiding me, Corporal.

I'm not a corporal, Brick answers. You know that. I've never been a soldier in my life.

Not in your world, Frisk says, but in this world you're a corporal in the Massachusetts Seventh, a member of the armed forces of the Independent States of America.

Putting his head in his hands, Brick groans softly as another element of the dream comes back to him: Worcester,

Massachusetts. He looks up, watches Frisk settle into a chair across from him at the table, and says: I'm in Massachusetts, then. Is that what you're telling me?

Wellington, Massachusetts, Frisk nods. Formerly known as Worcester.

Brick pounds his fist on the table, finally giving vent to the rage that has been building inside him. I don't like this! he shouts. Someone's inside my head. Not even my dreams belong to me. My whole life has been stolen. Then, turning to Frisk and looking him directly in the eye, he yells at the top of his voice: Who's doing this to me?

Take it easy, Frisk says, patting Brick on the hand. You have every right to be confused. That's why I'm here. I'm the one who explains it to you, who sets things straight. We don't want you to suffer. If you'd come to me when you were supposed to, you never would have had that dream. Do you understand what I'm trying to tell you?

Not really, Brick says, in a more subdued voice.

Through the walls of the house, he catches the faint sound of the jeep's engine being turned on, and then the distant squeal of shifting gears as Virginia drives away.

Virginia? he asks.

What about her?

She just left, didn't she?

She has a lot of work to do, and our business doesn't concern her.

She didn't even say good-bye, Brick adds, reluctant to drop

the matter. There is hurt in his voice, as if he can't quite believe that she would ditch him in such an offhanded way.

Forget Virginia, Frisk says. We have more important things to talk about.

She said I was going back. Is that true?

Yes. But first I have to tell you why. Listen carefully, Brick, and then give me an honest answer. Putting his arms on the table, Frisk leans forward and says: Are we in the real world or not?

How should I know? Everything looks real. Everything sounds real. I'm sitting here in my own body, but at the same time I can't be here, can I? I belong somewhere else.

You're here, all right. And you belong somewhere else.

It can't be both. It has to be one or the other.

Is the name Giordano Bruno familiar to you?

No. Never heard of him.

A sixteenth-century Italian philosopher. He argued that if God is infinite, and if the powers of God are infinite, then there must be an infinite number of worlds.

I suppose that makes sense. Assuming you believe in God.

He was burned at the stake for that idea. But that doesn't mean he was wrong, does it?

Why ask me? I don't know the first thing about any of this. How can I have an opinion about something I don't understand?

Until you woke up in that hole the other day, your entire life had been spent in one world. But how could you be sure it was the only world?

Because . . . because it was the only world I ever knew.

But now you know another world. What does that suggest to you, Brick?

I don't follow.

There's no single reality, Corporal. There are many realities. There's no single world. There are many worlds, and they all run parallel to one another, worlds and anti-worlds, worlds and shadow-worlds, and each world is dreamed or imagined or written by someone in another world. Each world is the creation of a mind.

You're beginning to sound like Tobak. He said the war was in one man's head, and if that man was eliminated, the war would stop. That's about the most asinine thing I've ever heard.

Tobak might not be the brightest soldier in the army, but he was telling you the truth.

If you want me to believe a crazy thing like that, you'll have to prove it to me first.

All right, Frisk says, slapping his palms on the table, what about this? Without another word, he reaches under his sweater with his right hand and pulls out a three-by-five photograph from his shirt pocket. This is the culprit, he says, sliding the photo across the table to Brick.

Brick does no more than glance at the picture. It's a color snapshot of a man in his late sixties or early seventies sitting in a wheelchair in front of a white country house. A perfectly sympathetic-looking man, Brick notes, with spiky gray hair and a weathered face.

This doesn't prove anything, he says, thrusting the photo

back at Frisk. It's just a man. Any man. For all I know, he could be your uncle.

His name is August Brill, Frisk begins, but Brick cuts him off before he can say anything else.

Not according to Tobak. He said his name was Blake.

Blank.

Whatever.

Tobak isn't up on the latest intelligence reports. For a long time, Blank was our leading suspect, but then we crossed him off the list. Brill is the one. We're sure of that now.

Then show me the story. Reach into that bag of yours and pull out his manuscript and point to a sentence where my name is mentioned.

That's the problem. Brill doesn't write anything down. He's telling himself the story in his head.

How can you possibly know that?

A military secret. But we know, Corporal. Trust me.

Bullshit.

You want to go back, don't you? Well, this is the only way. If you don't accept the job, you'll be stuck here forever.

All right. Just for the sake of argument, imagine I shoot this man . . . this Brill. Then what happens? If he created your world, then the moment he's dead, you won't exist anymore.

He didn't invent this world. He only invented the war. And he invented you, Brick. Don't you understand that? This is your story, not ours. The old man invented you in order to kill him.

So now it's a suicide.

In a roundabout way, yes.

Once again, Brick puts his head in his hands and begins to moan. It's all too much for him, and after struggling to hold his ground against Frisk's demented assertions, he can feel his mind dissolving, whirling madly through a universe of disconnected thoughts and amorphous dreads. Only one thing is clear to him: he wants to go back. He wants to be with Flora again and return to his old life. In order to do that, he must accept a command to murder someone he has never met, a total stranger. He will have to accept, but once he gets to the other side, what is to prevent him from refusing to carry out the job?

Still looking down at the table, he forces the words out of his mouth: Tell me something about the man.

Ah, that's better, Frisk says. Coming to our senses at last.

Don't patronize me, Frisk. Just tell me what I need to know.

A retired book critic, seventy-two years old, living outside Brattleboro, Vermont, with his forty-seven-year-old daughter and twenty-three-year-old granddaughter. His wife died last year. The daughter's husband left her five years ago. The granddaughter's boyfriend was killed. It's a house of grieving, wounded souls, and every night Brill lies awake in the dark, trying not to think about his past, making up stories about other worlds.

Why is he in a wheelchair?

A car accident. His left leg was shattered. They nearly had to amputate.

And if I agree to kill this man, you'll send me back.

That's the bargain. But don't try to wriggle out of it, Brick. If you break your promise, we'll come after you. Two bullets. One for you and one for Flora. Bang, bang. No more you. No more her.

But if you get rid of me, the war goes on.

Not necessarily. It's still just a hypothesis at this point, but some of us think that getting rid of you would produce the same result as eliminating Brill. The story would end, and the war would be over. Don't think we wouldn't be willing to take the risk.

How do I get back?

In your sleep.

But I've already gone to sleep here. Twice. And both times I woke up in the same place.

That's normal sleep. What I'm talking about is pharmacologically induced sleep. You'll be given an injection. The effect is similar to anesthesia—when they put a person under before surgery. The black void of oblivion, a nothingness as deep and dark as death.

Sounds like fun, Brick says, so unnerved by what is facing him that he can't help cracking a feeble joke.

Are you willing to give it a shot, Corporal?

Do I have a choice?

I feel a cough gathering in my chest, a faint rattle of phlegm buried deep in my bronchia, and before I can suppress it, the detonation comes blasting through my throat. Hack it up, propel the gunk northward, dislodge the slimy leftovers trapped in the tubes, but one try isn't enough, nor two, nor three, and here I am in a full-blown spasm, my whole body convulsing from the onslaught. It's my own fault. I stopped smoking fifteen years ago, but now that Katya is in the house with her ubiquitous American Spirits, I've begun to lapse into the old, dirty pleasures, cadging butts off her while we plunge through the entire corpus of world cinema, side by side on the sofa, blowing smoke in tandem, two locomotives chugging away from the loathsome, intolerable world, but without regret, I might add, without a second thought or single pang of remorse. It's the companionship that counts, the conspiratorial bond, the fuck-you solidarity of the damned.

Thinking about the films again, I realize that I have another example to add to Katya's list. I must remember to tell her first thing tomorrow morning—in the dining room over breakfast— since it's bound to please her, and if I can manage to coax a smile out of that glum face of hers, I'll consider it a worthy accomplishment.

The watch at the end of *Tokyo Story*. We saw the film a few days ago, the second time for both of us, but my first viewing goes decades back, the late sixties or early seventies, and other than remembering that I'd liked it, most of the story had vanished from my mind. Ozu, 1953, eight years after the Japanese defeat. A slow, stately film that tells the simplest of stories, but executed with such elegance and depth of feeling that I had tears in my eyes at the end. Some films are as good as books, as good as the best books (yes, Katya, I'll grant you that), and this is one of them, no question about it, a work as subtle and moving as a Tolstoy novella.

An aging couple travels to Tokyo to visit their grown-up children: a struggling doctor with a wife and children of his own, a married hairdresser who runs a beauty salon, and a daughter-in-law who was married to another son killed in the war, a young widow who lives alone and works in an office. From the beginning, it's clear that the son and daughter consider the presence of their old parents something of a burden, an inconvenience. They're busy with their jobs, with their families, and they don't have time to take proper care of them. Only the daughter-in-law goes out of her way to show them any kindness. Eventually, the parents leave Tokyo and return to the place where they live (never mentioned, I believe, or else I blinked and missed it), and some weeks after that, without warning, without any premonitory illness, the mother dies. The action of the film then shifts to the family house in that unnamed city or town. The grown-up children from Tokyo come for the funeral, along with the daughter-in-law, Norika or Noriko, I can't remember, but let's say Noriko and stick with that. Then a second son shows up from somewhere else, and finally there's the youngest child of the group, who still lives at home, a woman in her early twenties who works as an elementary school teacher. One quickly understands that not only does she adore and admire Noriko, she prefers her to her own siblings. After the funeral, the family is sitting around a table eating lunch, and once again the son and daughter from Tokyo are busy, busy, busy, too wrapped up in their own preoccupations to offer their father much support. They begin looking at their watches and decide to return to Tokyo on the night express. The second brother decides to leave as well. There is nothing overtly cruel about their behavior—this should be emphasized; it's in fact the essential point Ozu is making. They're merely distracted, caught up in the business of their own lives, and other responsibilities are pulling them away. But the gentle Noriko stays on, not wanting to abandon her grieving father-in-law (a walled-off, stone-faced grief, to be sure, but grief for all that), and on the last morning of her extended visit, she and the schoolteacher daughter have breakfast together.

The girl is still irritated by the hasty departure of her brothers and sister. She says they should have stayed longer and calls them selfish, but Noriko defends what they did (even if she would never do it herself), explaining that all children drift away from their parents in the end, that they have their own lives to look after. The girl insists that she'll never be like that. What's the point of a family if you act that way? she says. Noriko reiterates her previous comment, trying to comfort the girl by telling her that these things happen to children, that they can't be helped. A long pause follows, and then the girl looks at her sister-in-law and says: Life is disappointing, isn't it? Noriko looks back at the girl, and with a distant expression on her face, she answers: Yes, it is.

The teacher goes off to work, and Noriko begins straightening up the house (reminding me of the women in the other films Katya talked about tonight), and then comes the scene with the watch, the moment the entire film has been building up to. The old man walks into the house from the garden, and Noriko tells him she's leaving on the afternoon train. They sit down and talk, and if I can more or less remember the gist and flow of their conversation, it's because I asked Katya to play the scene again after the movie was finished. I was that impressed by it, and I wanted to study the dialogue more closely to see how Ozu managed to pull it off.

The old man begins by thanking her for everything she's done, but Noriko shakes her head and says she hasn't done anything. The old man presses on, telling her that she's been a great help and that his wife had talked to him about how kind she'd been to her. Again, Noriko resists the compliment, shrugging off her actions as unimportant, negligible. Not to be deterred, the old man says that his wife told him that being with Noriko was the happiest time she had in Tokyo. She was so worried about your future, he continues. You can't go on like this. You have to get married again. Forget about X (his son, her husband). He's dead.

Noriko is too upset to respond, but the old man isn't about to give up and let the conversation end. Referring to his wife again, he adds: She said you were the nicest woman she'd ever met. Noriko holds her ground, claiming that his wife overestimated her, but the old man bluntly tells her that she's wrong. Noriko is beginning to grow unhinged. I'm not the nice woman you think I am, she says. Really, I'm quite selfish. And then she explains that she isn't always thinking about the old man's son, that days go by and he doesn't even cross her mind once. After a little pause, she confesses how lonely she is and how, when she can't sleep at night, she lies in bed wondering what will become of her. My heart seems to be waiting for something, she says. I'm selfish.

OLD MAN: No, you're not.

NORIKO: Yes. I am.

OLD MAN: You're a good woman. An honest woman.

NORIKO: Not at all.

At that point, Noriko finally breaks down and begins to cry, sobbing into her hands as the floodgates open—this young woman who has suffered in silence for so long, this good woman who refuses to believe she's good, for only the good doubt their own goodness, which is what makes them good in the first place. The bad know they are good, but the good know nothing. They spend their lives forgiving others, but they can't forgive themselves.

The old man stands up, and a few seconds later he returns with the watch, an old-fashioned timepiece with a metal cover protecting the face. It belonged to his wife, he tells Noriko, and he wants her to have it. Accept it for her sake, he says. I'm sure she'd be glad.

Moved by the gesture, Noriko thanks him as the tears continue to roll down her cheeks. The old man studies her with a thoughtful look on his face, but those thoughts are impenetrable to us, since all his emotions are hidden behind a mask of somber neutrality. Watching Noriko cry, he then makes a simple declaration, delivering his words in such a forthright, unsentimental manner that they cause her to collapse in a fresh outburst of sobbing—prolonged, wrenching sobs, a cry of misery so deep and painful, it's as if the innermost core of her self has been cracked open.

I want you to be happy, the old man says.

One brief sentence, and Noriko falls apart, crushed by the weight of her own life. *I want you to be happy.* As she goes on crying, the father-in-law makes one more comment before the scene ends. It's strange, he says, almost in disbelief. We have children of our own, and yet you're the one who's done the most for us.

Cut to the school. We hear children singing, and a moment later we are in the daughter's classroom. The sound of a train is heard in the distance. The young woman looks at her watch and then walks to the window. A train roars by: the afternoon express, carrying her beloved sister-in-law back to Tokyo.

Cut to the train itself—and the thunderous noise of the wheels as they charge along the tracks. We are hurtling forward into the future.

A few moments after that, we are inside one of the carriages. Noriko is sitting alone, staring blankly into space, her mind elsewhere. Several more moments pass, and then she lifts her mother-in-law's watch off her lap. She opens the cover, and suddenly we can hear the second hand ticking around the dial. Noriko goes on examining the watch, the expression on her face at once sad and contemplative, and as we look at her with the watch in the palm of her hand, we feel that we are looking at time itself, time speeding ahead as the train speeds ahead, pushing us forward into life and then more life, but also time as the past, the dead mother-in-law's past, Noriko's past, the past

that lives on in the present, the past we carry with us into the future.

The shriek of a train whistle resounds in our ears, a cruel and piercing noise. *Life is disappointing, isn't it?*

I want you to be happy.

And then the scene abruptly ends.

Widows. Women living alone. An image of the sobbing Noriko in my head. Impossible not to think of my sister now—and the luckless hand she was dealt by marrying a man who died young. It's been brewing in me ever since I started thinking about my civil war: the fact that in my own life I've been spared from all things military. An accident of birth, the fluke of entering the world in 1935, which made me too young for Korea and too old for Vietnam, and then the further good fortune to have been rejected by the army when I was drafted in 1957. They said I had a heart murmur, which turned out not to be true, and classified me as 4-F. No wars, then, but the time I came closest to something that resembled one, I happened to be with Betty and her second husband, Gilbert Ross. It was 1967, exactly forty years ago this summer, and the three of us were having dinner together on the Upper East Side, Lexington Avenue I think it was, Sixty-sixth or Sixty-seventh Street, in a long-gone Chinese restaurant called Sun Luck. Sonia had gone off to France to visit her parents outside Lyon with the seven-year-old Miriam. I was supposed to join them later, but for the time being I was holed up in our shoe box of an apartment off

Riverside Drive, sweating out a long piece for *Harper's* on recent American poetry and fiction inspired by the Vietnam war—with no air conditioner, just a cheap plastic fan, scribbling and typing in my underwear as my pores gushed through another New York heat wave. Money was tight for us back then, but Betty was seven years older than I was and living comfortably, as they say, and therefore she was in a position to invite her kid brother out for a free dinner every now and then. After a bad first marriage that had lasted too long, she had married Gil about three years earlier. A wise choice, I felt—or at least it looked that way at the time. Gil earned his money as a labor lawyer and strike mediator, but he had also joined the Newark city government as corporation counsel in the early sixties, and when he and my sister came to New York that night forty years ago, he was driving a city car, which was equipped with a two-way radio. I can't remember a thing about the dinner itself, but when we walked back to the car and Gil started up the engine to drive me home, frantic voices came pouring through the radio—police calls, I presume, reporting that the Central Ward of Newark was in chaos. Without bothering to go uptown to drop me at my apartment, Gil headed straight for the Lincoln Tunnel, and that was how I came to witness one of the worst race riots in American history. More than twenty people killed, more than seven hundred people injured, more than fifteen hundred people arrested, more than ten million dollars in property damage. I remember these numbers because when Katya was in high school a few years ago, she wrote a paper on racism for her American history

class, and she interviewed me about the riot. Odd that those figures should have stuck, but with so many other things slipping away from me now, I cling to them as proof that I'm not quite finished.

Driving into Newark that night was like entering one of the lower circles of hell. Buildings in flames, hordes of men running wildly through the streets, the noise of shattering glass as one store window after another was broken, the noise of sirens, the noise of gunshots. Gil drove to City Hall, and once the three of us were inside the building, we went directly to the mayor's office. Sitting at his desk was Hugh Addonizio, a bald, bulging, pear-shaped man in his mid-fifties, ex–war hero, six-time congressman, in his second term as mayor, and the big man was utterly lost, sitting at his desk with tears pouring down his face. What am I going to do? he said, looking up at Gil. What the hell am I going to do?

An indelible picture, undimmed after all these years: the sight of that pathetic figure paralyzed by the pressure of events, a man gone rigid with despair as the city exploded around him. Meanwhile, Gil calmly went about his business, calling the governor in Trenton, calling the chief of police, doing his best to get a grip on the situation. At one point, he and I left the room and went downstairs to the jail on the bottom floor of the building. The cells were crammed with prisoners, every one of them a black man, and at least half of them stood there with their clothes torn, blood trickling from their heads, their faces swollen. It wasn't difficult to guess what had caused these wounds, but Gil asked the question anyway. Man by

man, the answer never varied: each one had been beaten by the cops.

Not long after we returned to the mayor's office, in walked a member of the New Jersey State Police, a certain Colonel Brand or Brandt, a man of around forty with a razor-sharp crew cut, a square, clenched jaw, and the hard eyes of a marine about to embark on a commando mission. He shook hands with Addonizio, sat down in a chair, and then pronounced these words: We're going to hunt down every black bastard in this city. I probably shouldn't have been shocked, but I was. Not by the statement, perhaps, but by the chilling contempt of the voice that uttered it. Gil told him not to use that kind of language, but the colonel merely sighed and shook his head, dismissing my brother-in-law's remark as if he considered him to be an ignorant fool.

That was my war. Not a real war, perhaps, but once you witness violence on that scale, it isn't difficult to imagine something worse, and once your mind is capable of doing that, you understand that the worst possibilities of the imagination are the country you live in. Just think it, and chances are it will happen.

That fall, when Gil was put in the untenable position of having to defend the city of Newark against scores of lawsuits from shopkeepers whose businesses had been destroyed in the riot, he quit his post and never worked in government again. Fifteen years later, two months short of his fifty-third birthday, he was dead.

I want to think about Betty, but in order to do that I have to

think about Gil, and to think about Gil I have to go back to the beginning. And yet, how much do I know? Not a lot, finally, no more than a few pertinent facts, gleaned from stories he and Betty told me. The first of three children born to a Newark saloonkeeper who supposedly could have passed as Babe Ruth's double. At some point, Dutch Schultz muscled in on Gil's father and stole the business, how or why I can't say, and a few years after that his father dropped dead of a heart attack. Gil was eleven at the time, and since his father died broke, the only thing he inherited from him was chronic high blood pressure and heart disease—which was first diagnosed at age eighteen and then blossomed into a full-blown coronary when he was just thirty-four, followed by another one two years later. Gil was a tall, powerful man, but he spent his whole life with a death sentence circulating in his veins.

His mother remarried when he was thirteen, and while his stepfather had no objections to raising the two younger kids, he wanted no part of Gil and kicked him out of the house— with the mother's consent. Talk about the unimaginable: to be exiled by your own mother and sent off to live with relatives in Florida for the rest of your childhood.

After high school, he came back north and started college at NYU, strapped for money, forced to work several part-time jobs to keep himself afloat. Once, when he was reminiscing about how hard up he was in those days, he described how he used to go to Ratner's, the old Jewish dairy restaurant on the Lower East Side, sit down at a table, and tell the waiter that he was expecting his girlfriend to show up at any minute. One of the chief lures of the place was the celebrated Ratner's dinner roll. The moment you took your seat, a waiter would come over and plunk down a basket of those rolls in front of you, accompanied by an ample supply of butter. Roll by buttered roll, Gil would eat his way through the basket, glancing at his watch from time to time, pretending to be upset by the lateness of his nonexistent girlfriend. Once the first basket was empty, it would automatically be replaced by a second, and then the second by a third. Finally, the girlfriend would fail to appear, and Gil would leave the restaurant with a disappointed look on his face. After a while, the waiters caught on to the trick, but not before Gil achieved a personal record of twenty-seven free rolls consumed at a single sitting.

Law school, followed by the start of a successful practice and a growing involvement with the Democratic Party. Idealistic, left-wing liberalism, a supporter of Stevenson for the 1960 presidential nomination, Eleanor Roosevelt's escort at the convention in Atlantic City, and later a photograph (which I've owned since Betty's death) of Gil shaking hands with John F. Kennedy during a visit to Newark in 1962 or 1963 as Kennedy said to him: We've been hearing great things about you. But all that turned sour after the Newark disaster, and once Gil left politics, he and Betty packed it in and moved to California. I didn't see much of them after that, but for the next six or seven years I gathered all was calm. Gil built up his law practice, my sister opened a store in Laguna Beach (kitchenware, table linens, top-quality grinders and gadgets), and even though Gil had to swallow more than twenty pills a day to keep himself

alive, whenever they came east for family visits, he looked
to be in good shape. Then his health turned. By the mid-
seventies, a series of cardiac arrests and other debilitations
made work all but impossible for him. I sent them whatever I
could whenever I could, and with Betty working full-time to
keep them going, Gil now spent most of his days alone in the
house, reading books. My big sister and her dying husband,
three thousand miles away from me. During those last years,
Betty told me, Gil would plant love notes in the drawers of her
bureau, hiding them among her bras and slips and panties,
and every morning when she woke up and got dressed, she
would find another billet-doux declaring that she was the most
gorgeous woman in the world. Not bad, finally. Considering
what they were up against, not bad at all.

I don't want to think about the end: the cancer, the final
stay in the hospital, the obscene sunlight that flooded the
cemetery on the morning of the funeral. I've already dredged
up enough, but still, I can't let go of this without revisiting one
last detail, one last ugly turn. By the time Gil died, Betty was
so deeply in debt that paying for a burial plot was a genuine
hardship. I was prepared to help, but she had already asked
me for money so often that she couldn't bring herself to do it
again. Rather than turn to me, she went to her mother-in-law,
the infamous woman who had allowed Gil to be thrown out of
the house when he was a boy. I can't remember her name
(probably because I despised her so much), but by 1980 she
was married to her third husband, a retired businessman who
happened to be immensely rich. As for husband number two,

I don't know if his departure was caused by death or divorce—
but no matter. Rich husband number three owned a large family plot in a cemetery somewhere in southern Florida, and my
sister managed to talk him into letting Gil be buried there.
Less than a year after that, husband number three died, and a
large, Balzacian inheritance war broke out between his children and Gil's mother. They took her to court, won their case,
and in order for her to come out of the affair with any money at
all, one of the conditions of the settlement required that Gil's
remains be removed from the family plot. Imagine. The woman
evicts her son from his house when he's a child, and then, for
a bag of silver, evicts him from his grave after he's dead. When
Betty called to tell me what had happened, she was sobbing.
She had held up through Gil's death with a kind of grim, stoic
grace, but this was too much for her, and she broke down and
lost it completely. By the time Gil was exhumed and buried
again, she was no longer the same person.

She lasted another four years. Living alone in a small
apartment in the New Jersey suburbs, she grew fat, then very
fat, and before long came down with diabetes, clogged arter-
ies, and a thick dossier of other ailments. She held my hand
when Oona left me and our catastrophic five-year marriage
ended, applauded when Sonia and I got back together, saw
her son whenever he and his wife flew in from Chicago, at-
tended family events, watched television from morning to
night, could still tell a decent joke when the spirit moved her,
and turned into the saddest person I have ever known. One
morning in the spring of 1987, her housekeeper called me in a

state of quasi-hysteria. She had just entered Betty's apartment, using the key she had been given for her weekly cleaning chores, and had found my sister lying on the bed. I borrowed a car from a neighbor, drove out to New Jersey, and identified her body for the police. The shock of seeing her like that: so still, so far away, so terribly, terribly dead. When they asked me if I wanted the hospital to conduct an autopsy, I told them not to bother. There were only two possibilities. Either her body had given out on her or she had taken pills, and I didn't want to know the answer, for neither one of them would have told the real story. Betty died of a broken heart. Some people laugh when they hear that phrase, but that's because they don't know anything about the world. People die of broken hearts. It happens every day, and it will go on happening to the end of time.

No, I haven't forgotten. The cough sent me spinning into another zone, but I'm back now, and Brick is still with me. Through thick and thin, in spite of that dismal excursion into the past, but how to stop the mind from charging off wherever it wants to go? The mind has a mind of its own. Who said that? Someone, or else I just thought of it myself, not that it makes any difference. Coining phrases in the middle of the night, making up stories in the middle of the night—we're moving on, my little darlings, and agonizing as this mess can be, there's poetry in it, too, as long as you can find the words to express it, assuming those words exist. Yes, Miriam, life is disappointing. But I also want you to be happy.

Fret not. I'm treading water because I can see the story turning in any one of several directions, and I still haven't decided which path to take. Hope or no hope? Both options are available, and yet neither one is fully satisfying to me. Is there a middle way after such a beginning, after throwing Brick to the wolves and bending the poor sap's mind out of shape? Probably not. Think dark, then, and go down into it, see it through to the end.

The injection has already been given. Brick falls into the bottomless black of unconsciousness, and hours later he opens his eyes and discovers that he's in bed with Flora. It's early morning, seven-thirty or eight o'clock, and as Brick looks at the naked back of his sleeping wife, he wonders if he wasn't right all along, if the time he spent in Wellington wasn't part of some bad, nauseatingly vivid dream. But then, as he shifts his head on the pillow, he feels Virginia's bandage pressing into his cheek, and when he runs his tongue over the ragged edge of his chipped incisor, he has no choice but to face the facts: he was there, and everything that happened to him in that place was real. By now, there is only a single, improbable straw to clutch at: what if the two days that elapsed in Wellington were no more than a blink of the eyes in this world? What if Flora never knew he was gone? That would solve the problem of having to explain where he's been, for Brick knows the truth will be difficult to swallow, especially for a jealous woman like Flora, and yet even if the truth comes out sounding like a lie, he doesn't have the strength or the will to concoct a story that would seem more plausible, something that would appease her suspicions and make her understand that his two-day absence had nothing to do with another woman.

Unfortunately for Brick, the clocks in both worlds tell the same time. Flora knows that he's been missing, and when she turns over in her sleep and inadvertently touches his body, she is instantly jolted awake. His anxieties are stilled by the joy that comes rushing into her intense brown eyes, and suddenly he feels ashamed of himself, mortified that he ever could have doubted her love for him.

Owen? she asks, as if hardly daring to believe what has happened. Is it really you?

Yes, Flora, he says. I'm back.

She throws her arms around him, holding him tightly against her smooth, bare skin. I've been going *crazy,* she says, rolling the *r* with an emphatic trilling of her tongue. Just *crazy* out of my head. Then, as she sees the bandage on his cheek and the bruises around his lips, her expression changes to one of alarm. What happened? she asks. You're all beat up, baby.

It takes him over an hour to give a full account of his mysterious journey to the other America. The only thing he leaves out is Virginia's last remark about wanting to charm his pants off and fuck his brains out, but that is a minor detail, and he sees no point in riling up Flora with matters that have little bearing on the story. The most daunting part comes toward the end, when he tries to recapitulate his conversation with Frisk. It barely made sense to him at the time, and now that he's back in his own apartment, sitting in the kitchen and drinking coffee with his wife, all that talk about multiple realities and multiple worlds dreamed and imagined by other minds strikes him as out-and-out gibberish. He shakes his head, as if to apologize for making such a botch of it. But the injection was real, he says. And the order to shoot August Brill was real. And if he doesn't carry out the job, he and Flora will be in constant danger.

Until now, Flora has listened in silence, patiently watching her husband tell his absurd and ridiculous story, which she considers to be the largest mound of crap ever built by human hands. Under normal circumstances, she would fly into one of her rages and accuse him of two-timing her, but these are not normal circumstances, and Flora, who knows every one of Brick's faults, who has criticized him countless times during the three years of their marriage, has never once called him a liar, and in the face of the nonsense she has just been told, she finds herself stunned, at a loss for words.

I know it sounds incredible, Brick says. But it's all true, every word of it.

And you expect me to believe you, Owen?

I can hardly believe it myself. But it all happened, Flora, exactly as I told it to you.

Do you think I'm an idiot?

What are you talking about?

Either you think I'm an idiot or you've gone insane.

I don't think you're an idiot, and I haven't gone insane.

You sound like one of those crackpots. You know, one of

those guys who's been abducted by aliens. What did the Martians look like, Owen? Did they have a big spaceship?

Stop it, Flora. That isn't funny.

Funny? Who's trying to be funny? I just want to know where you've been.

I've already told you. Don't think I wasn't tempted to make up another story. Some stupid thing about getting mugged and losing my memory for two days. Or being run over by a car. Or falling down the stairs in the subway. Some drek like that. But I decided to tell you the truth.

Maybe that's it. You got beat up, after all. Maybe you've been lying in an alley for the past two days, and you dreamed the whole thing.

Then why would I have this on my arm? A nurse put it there after they gave me the shot. It's the last thing I remember before I opened my eyes this morning.

Brick rolls up his left sleeve, points to a small flesh-colored bandage on his upper arm, and tears it off with his right hand. Look, he says. Do you see this little scab? That's the spot where the needle went into my skin.

It doesn't mean anything, Flora replies, dismissing the one piece of solid evidence Brick can offer. There are a million different ways you could have gotten that scab.

True. But the fact is it happened just one way, the way I told you. From Frisk's needle.

All right, Owen, Flora says, trying not to lose her temper, maybe we should stop talking about it now. You're home. That's the only thing that matters to me. Christ, baby, you don't know what it was like for those two days. I went nuts, I mean one hundred percent nuts. I thought you were dead. I thought you'd left me. I thought you were with another girl. And now you're back. It's like a miracle, and if you want to know the truth, I don't really care what happened. You were gone, and now you're back. End of story, okay?

No, Flora, it's not okay. I'm back, but the story isn't over. I have to go up to Vermont and shoot Brill. I don't know how much time I have, but I can't sit around and wait too long. If I don't do it, they're going to come after us. A bullet for you and a bullet for me. That's what Frisk said, and he wasn't joking.

Brill, Flora grunts, pronouncing the name as if it were an insult in some foreign language. I bet he doesn't even exist.

I saw his picture, remember?

A picture doesn't prove anything.

That's exactly what I said when Frisk showed it to me.

Well, there's one way to find out, isn't there? If he's some kind of hotshot writer, he has to be on the Internet. Let's turn on my computer and look him up.

Frisk said he won a Pulitzer Prize about twenty years ago. If his name isn't on the list, then we're home free. If it is, then watch out, little Flora. We're in for some big trouble.

It won't be, Owen. Count on it. Brill doesn't exist, so his name can't be there.

But it is there. August Brill, winner of the 1984 Pulitzer Prize for criticism. They look further, and within minutes they have uncovered vast amounts of information, including biographical data from *Who's Who in America* (born NYC, 1935;

married Sonia Weil, 1957, divorced 1975; married Oona
McNally, 1976, divorced 1981; daughter, Miriam, born 1960;
B.A. from Columbia, 1957; honorary doctorates from Williams
College and the Pratt Institute; member of the American
Academy of Arts and Sciences; author of more than 1,500 articles, reviews, and columns for magazines and newspapers;
book editor of the *Boston Globe,* 1972–1991), a Web site con-
taining over four hundred of his pieces written between 1962
and 2003, as well as a number of photographs taken of Brill in
his thirties, forties, and fifties, leaving no doubt that these are
younger versions of the old man in the wheelchair parked in
front of the white clapboard house in Vermont.

Brick and Flora are sitting side by side at a small desk in
the bedroom, their eyes fixed on the screen in front of them,
too afraid to look at each other as they watch their hopes turn
to dust. At last, Flora switches off the laptop and says in a low,
quavering voice: I guess I was wrong, huh?

Brick stands up and begins pacing around the room. Do you
believe me now? he asks. This Brill, this goddamn August
Brill . . . I'd never even heard of him until yesterday. How
could I have made it up? I'm not smart enough to have thought
of half the things I've told you, Flora. I'm just a guy who performs magic tricks for little kids. I don't read books, I don't
know anything about book critics, and I'm not interested in politics. Don't ask me how, but I've just come from a place that's in
the middle of a civil war. And now I have to kill a man.

He sits down on the edge of the bed, overwhelmed by the
ferocity of his situation, by the sheer injustice of what has

happened to him. Watching Brick with worried eyes, Flora walks across the room and sits down beside him. She puts her arms around her husband, leans her head against his shoulder, and says: You're not going to kill anyone.

I have to, Brick answers, staring down at the floor.

I don't know what to think or not to think, Owen, but I'm telling you now, you're not going to kill anyone. You're going to leave that man alone.

I can't.

Why do you think I married you? Because you're a sweet person, my love, a kind and honest person. I didn't marry a killer. I married you, my funny Owen Brick, and I'm not going to stand by and let you murder someone and spend the rest of your life in prison.

I'm not saying I want to do it. I just don't have any choice.

Don't talk like that. Everyone has a choice. And besides, what makes you think you'd be able to go through with it? Can you actually see yourself walking into that man's house, pointing a gun at his head, and shooting him in cold blood? Not in a hundred years, Owen. It's just not in you to do something like that. Thank God.

Brick knows that Flora is right. He could never kill an innocent stranger, not even if his own life depended on it—which it probably does. He lets out a long, shuddering breath, then runs his hand through Flora's hair and says: So what am I supposed to do?

Nothing.

What do you mean, *nothing*?

We start living again. You do your job, I do mine. We eat and sleep and pay the bills. We wash the dishes and vacuum the floor. We make a baby together. You put me in the bath and shampoo my hair. I rub your back. You learn new tricks. We visit your parents and listen to your mother complain about her health. We go on, baby, and live our little life. That's what I'm talking about. Nothing.

A month goes by. In the first week after Brick's return, Flora misses her period, and a home pregnancy test brings them the news that if all goes well, they will become parents by the following January. They celebrate the positive test result by going out to a fashionable Manhattan restaurant that is far beyond their means, consume an entire bottle of French champagne before placing their orders, and then gorge themselves on a gargantuan porterhouse for two, which Flora claims is almost as good as the meat in Argentina. The next day, on his second visit to the dentist, a cap is put on Brick's left incisor, and he resumes his career as the Great Zavello. Bolting around the city in his battered yellow Mazda, he dons his cape and performs at elementary school assemblies, retirement homes, community centers, and private parties, pulling doves and rabbits out of his top hat, making silk scarves disappear, snatching eggs out of thin air, and transforming dull newspapers into colorful bouquets of pansies, tulips, and roses. Flora, who left her catering job two years earlier and is now working as a receptionist at a doctor's office on Park Avenue, asks her boss for a twenty-dollar raise and is turned down. She explodes in a tantrum of injured pride and storms out of the building, but when she talks it over with Brick that evening, he persuades her to return the next morning and apologize to Dr. Sontag, which she does, and because the doctor doesn't want to lose such a competent, hardworking employee, he rewards her with a ten-dollar increase in salary, which is all she was hoping for in the first place. Money is nevertheless an issue, and with a child now on the way, Brick and Flora wonder if they will be able to feed that third mouth with what they are earning now. On a grim Sunday afternoon toward the end of the month, they even discuss the possibility of Brick going to work for his cousin Ralph, who owns a high-powered real estate agency in Park Slope. Magic would have to become a part-time occupation, little more than a hobby to be pursued on his days off, and Brick is reluctant to take such a drastic step, vowing to land some higher-paying jobs that will give them the breathing room they need. Meanwhile, he has not forgotten his visit to the other America. Wellington is still burning inside him, and not a day goes by when he doesn't think of Tobak, Molly Wald, Duke Rothstein, Frisk, and, most disturbingly of all, Virginia Blaine. He can't help himself. Flora has been so much more tender with him since his return, metamorphosing herself into the loving companion he always longed for, and while there is no question that he loves her back, Virginia is always there, lurking in a corner of his mind, gently putting the bandage on his face and telling him how much she wanted to charm his pants off. By way of compensation, perhaps, he begins reading Brill's old reviews on the Internet—always in secret, of course, since he doesn't want

Flora to know that he's still thinking about the man he was instructed to kill—and every time he comes across an article about a book that sounds interesting, he checks it out of the library. He used to spend his evenings watching television with Flora on a sofa in the living room. Now he lies on the bed and reads books. So far, his most important discoveries have been Chekhov, Calvino, and Camus.

In this way Brick and Flora swim along in their conjugal nothing, the little life she lured him back to with the good sense of a woman who doesn't believe in other worlds, who knows there is only this world and that numbing routines and brief squabbles and financial worries are an essential part of it, that in spite of the aches and boredoms and disappointments, living in this world is the closest we will ever come to seeing paradise. After the horrific hours he spent in Wellington, Brick too wants only this, the jumbled grind of New York, the naked body of his little Floratina, his work as the Great Zavello, his unborn child growing invisibly as the days pass, and yet deep inside himself he knows that he has been contaminated by his visit to the other world and that sooner or later everything will come to an end. He contemplates driving up to Vermont and talking to Brill. Would it be possible to convince the old man to stop thinking about his story? He tries to imagine the conversation, tries to summon the words he would use to present his argument, but all he ever sees is Brill laughing at him, the incredulous laughter of a man who would take him for an imbecile, a mental defective, and promptly throw him out of the house. So Brick does nothing, and precisely one month after his return from Wellington, on the evening of May twenty-first, as he sits in the living room with Flora, demonstrating a new card trick to his laughing wife, someone knocks on the door. Without having to think about it, Brick already knows what has happened. He tells Flora not to open the door, to run into the bedroom and go down the fire escape as fast as she can, but willful, independent Flora, unaware of the fix they're in, scoffs at his panicked instructions and does exactly what he tells her not to do. Bounding off the sofa before he can grab her arm, she dances to the door with a mocking pirouette and yanks it open. Two men are standing on the threshold, Lou Frisk and Duke Rothstein, and since each one is holding a revolver in his hand and pointing it at Flora, Brick doesn't move from his spot on the sofa. Theoretically, he can still try to escape, but the moment he stood up, the mother of his child would be dead.

Who the fuck are you? Flora says, in a shrill, angry voice.

Sit down next to your husband, Frisk replies, waving his gun in the direction of the sofa. We have some business to discuss with him.

Turning to Brick with an anguished look on her face, Flora says: What's going on, baby?

Come here, Brick answers, patting the sofa with his right hand. Those guns aren't toys, and you have to do what they say.

For once, Flora doesn't resist, and as the two men enter the apartment and shut the door, she walks over to the sofa and sits down beside her husband.

These are my friends, Brick says to her. Duke Rothstein

and Lou Frisk. Remember when I told you about them? Well, here they are.

Jesus holy Christ, Flora mutters, by now sick to death with fear.

Frisk and Rothstein settle into two chairs opposite the sofa. The cards that were used to demonstrate the trick are strewn across the surface of the coffee table in front of them. Taking hold of one of the cards and turning it over, Frisk says: I'm glad you remember us, Owen. We were beginning to have our doubts.

Don't worry, Brick says. I never forget a face.

How's the tooth? Rothstein asks, breaking into what looks like a cross between a grimace and a smile.

Much better, thank you, Brick says. I went to the dentist, and he put a cap on it.

I'm sorry I hit you so hard. But orders are orders, and I had to do my job. Scare tactics. I guess they didn't work too well, did they?

Have you ever had a gun pointed at you? Frisk asks.

Believe it or not, Brick says, this is the first time.

You seem to be handling it pretty well.

I've played it out in my head so often, I feel as if it's already happened.

Which means you've been expecting us.

Of course I've been expecting you. The only surprise is that you didn't show up sooner.

We figured we'd give you a month. It's a tough assignment, and it seemed only fair to give you a little time to work yourself up to it. But the month is over now, and we still haven't seen any results. Do you want to explain yourself?

I can't do it. That's all. I just can't do it.

While you've been twiddling your thumbs in Jackson Heights, the war has gone from bad to worse. The Federals launched a spring offensive, and nearly every town on the East Coast has been under attack. Operation Unity, they call it. A million and a half more dead while you sit here wrestling with your conscience. The Twin Cities were invaded three weeks ago, and half of Minnesota is under Federal control again. Huge parts of Idaho, Wyoming, and Nebraska have been turned into prison camps. Shall I go on?

No, no, I get the picture.

You have to do it, Brick.

I'm sorry. I just can't.

You remember the consequences, don't you?

Isn't that why you're here?

Not yet. We're giving you a deadline. One week from today. If Brill isn't taken care of by midnight on the twenty-eighth, Duke and I will be back, and next time our guns will be loaded. Do you hear me, Corporal? One week from today, or else you and your wife die for nothing.

I don't know what time it is. The hands on the alarm clock aren't illuminated, and I'm not about to switch on the lamp again and subject myself to the blinding rays of the bulb. I keep intending to ask Miriam to buy me one of those glow-in-the-dark jobs, but every time I wake up in the morning, I forget. The light erases the thought, and I don't remember it again until I'm back in bed, lying awake as I am now, staring up at the invisible ceiling in my invisible room. I can't be certain, but I would guess it's somewhere between one-thirty and two o'clock. Inching along, inching along . . .

The Web site was Miriam's idea. If I had known what she was up to, I would have told her not to waste her time, but she kept it a secret from me (in collusion with her mother, who had saved nearly every scrap of writing I'd ever published), and when she came to New York for my seventieth-birthday dinner, she took me into my study, turned on my laptop, and showed me what she had done. The articles were hardly worth the trouble, but the thought of my daughter spending untold hours typing up all those ancient pieces of mine—*for posterity,* as she put it—more or less undid me, and I didn't know what to say. My usual impulse is to deflect emotional scenes with a dry quip or wiseacre remark, but that night I simply put my arms around Miriam and said nothing. Sonia cried, of course. She always cried when she was happy, but on that occasion her tears were especially poignant and terrible to me, since her cancer had been detected only three days earlier and the prognosis was cloudy, touch-and-go at best. No one said a word about it, but all three of us knew that she might not be around for my next birthday. As it turned out, a year was too much to hope for.

I shouldn't be doing this. I promised myself not to fall into the trap of Sonia-thoughts and Sonia-memories, not to let myself go. I can't afford to break down now and sink into a despond of grief and self-recrimination. I might start howling and wake the girls upstairs—or else spend the next several hours thinking of ever more artful and devious ways to kill myself. That task has been reserved for Brick, the protagonist of tonight's story. Perhaps that explains why he and Flora turn on her computer and look at Miriam's Web site. It seems important that my hero should get to know me a bit, to learn what kind of man he's up against, and now that he's dipped into some of the books I've recommended, we've finally begun to establish a bond. It's turning into a rather complicated jig, I suppose, but the fact is that the Brill character wasn't in my original plan. The mind that created the war was going to belong to someone else, another invented character, as unreal as Brick and Flora and Tobak and all the rest, but the longer I went on, the more I understood how badly I was fooling myself. The story is about a man who must kill the person who created him, and why pretend that I am not that person? By putting myself into the story, the story becomes real. Or else I become unreal, yet one more figment of my own imagination. Either way, the effect is more satisfying, more in harmony with my mood—which is dark, my little ones, as dark as the obsidian night that surrounds me.

I'm blathering on, letting my thoughts fly helter-skelter to keep Sonia at bay, but in spite of my efforts, she's still there, the ever-present absent one, who spent so many nights in this bed with me, now lying in a grave in the Cimetière Montparnasse, my French wife of eighteen years, and then nine years apart, and then twenty-one more years together, thirty-nine years in all, forty-one counting the two years before our wedding, more than half my life, much more than half, and nothing left now but boxes of photographs and seven scratchy LPs, the recordings she made in the sixties and seventies, Schubert, Mozart, Bach, and the chance to listen to her voice again, that small but beautiful voice, so drenched in feeling, so much the essence of who she was. Photographs . . . and music . . . and Miriam. She left me our child, too, that mustn't be overlooked, the child who is no longer a child, and how strange to think that I'd be lost without her now, no doubt drunk every night, if not dead or on life support in some hospital. When she asked me to move in with her after the accident, I politely turned her down, explaining that she had enough burdens already without adding me to the list. She took hold of my hand and said: No, Dad, you don't get it. I need you. I'm so damned lonely in that house, I don't know how much longer I can take it. I need someone to talk to. I need someone to look at, to be there at dinner, to hold me every once in a while and tell me that I'm not an awful person.

Awful person must have come from Richard, an epithet that shot out of his mouth during an ugly row at the end of their marriage. People say the worst things in the flush of anger, and it pains me that Miriam allowed those words to stick to her like some ultimate judgment of her character, a condemnation of who and what she is. There are depths of goodness in that girl, the same kind of self-punishing goodness that Noriko embodies in the film, and because of that, almost inevitably, even if

Richard was the one who jumped ship, she continues to fault herself for what happened. I don't know if I've been of much help to her, but at least she isn't alone anymore. We were settling into a fairly comfortable routine before Titus was killed, and I just want you to remember this, Miriam: when Katya was in trouble, she didn't go to her father, she went to you.

By now, Frisk and Rothstein have left the apartment. The moment the door shuts behind them, Flora begins swearing in Spanish, reeling off a long spate of invective that Brick is unable to follow, since his knowledge of the language is limited to just a few words, principally *hello* and *good-bye,* and yet he doesn't interrupt her, withdrawing into himself during those thirty seconds of incomprehension to ponder the dilemma that is facing them and think of what to do next. He finds it odd, but all fear seems to have left him, and while just minutes earlier he was convinced that he and Flora were about to be killed, instead of shaking and trembling in the aftermath of that unexpected reprieve, a great calm has settled over him. He saw his death in the form of Frisk's gun, and even if that gun is no longer there, his death is still with him—as if it were the only thing that belonged to him now, as if whatever life remains in him has already been stolen by that death. And if Brick is doomed, then the first thing to be done is to protect Flora by sending her as far away from him as possible.

Brick is calm, but it seems to have no effect on his wife, who is growing more and more agitated.

What are we going to do? she says. My God, Owen, we can't just sit around here and wait for them to come back. I don't want to die. It's too stupid to die when you're twenty-seven years old. I don't know . . . maybe we can run away and hide somewhere.

It wouldn't do any good. Wherever we went, they're bound to track us down.

Then maybe you have to kill that old man, after all.

We've already been through that. You were against it, remember?

I didn't know anything then. Now I know.

I don't see how that makes any difference. I can't do it, and even if I could, I'd only wind up in prison.

Who says you'll be caught? If you think of a good plan, maybe you'll get away with it.

Leave it alone, Flora. You don't want me to do it any more than I do.

Okay. Then we hire someone to do it for you.

Stop it. We're not killing anyone. Do you understand me?

What then? If we don't do something, we'll be dead one week from tonight.

I'm going to send you away. That's the first step. Back to your mother in Buenos Aires.

But you just said they'd find us wherever we go.

They're not interested in you. I'm the one they're after, and once we're apart, they're not going to bother with you.

What are you saying, Owen?

Just that I want you to be safe.

And what about you?

Don't worry. I'll think of something. I'm not going to let myself be killed by those two maniacs, I promise. You'll go down and visit your mother for a while, and when you come back, I'll be waiting for you in this apartment. Understood?

I don't like it, Owen.

You don't have to like it. You just have to do it. For me.

That evening they book a round-trip flight to Buenos Aires, and the next morning Brick drives Flora to the airport. He knows it is the last time he will ever see her, but he struggles to maintain his composure and gives no hint of the anguish roiling inside him. As he kisses her good-bye at the security entrance, surrounded by throngs of travelers and uniformed airport personnel, Flora suddenly begins to cry. Brick gathers her into his arms and strokes the top of her head, but now that he can feel her body convulsing against his, and now that her tears are seeping through his shirt and dampening his skin, he no longer knows what to say.

Don't make me go, Flora begs.

No tears, he whispers back to her. It's only ten days. By the time you come home, everything will be finished.

And so it will, he thinks, as he climbs into his car and drives home to Jackson Heights from the airport. At that point, he has every intention of keeping his word: to avoid another encounter with Rothstein and Frisk, to be waiting for Flora in the apartment when she returns—but that doesn't mean he plans on being alive.

So now it's a suicide, he remembers saying to Frisk.

In a roundabout way, yes.

Brick is approaching his thirtieth birthday, and not once in his life has he ever thought of killing himself. Now it has become his sole preoccupation, and for the next two days he sits in the apartment trying to figure out the most painless and efficient method of leaving this world. He considers buying a gun and shooting himself in the head. He considers poison. He considers slitting his wrists. Yes, he says to himself, that's the old standard, isn't it? Drink half a bottle of vodka, pour twenty or thirty sleeping pills down your throat, slip into a warm tub, and then slash your veins with a carving knife. Rumor has it that you barely feel a thing.

The conundrum is that there are still five more days to go, and with each day that passes, the calm and certainty that descended over his mind as he looked into the barrel of Frisk's gun loosen their hold on him by several more degrees. Death was a foregone conclusion back then, a mere formality under the circumstances, but as his calm gradually turns into disquiet, and his certainty melts away into doubt, he tries to imagine the vodka and the pills, the warm bath and the blade of the knife, and suddenly the old fear returns, and once that happens, he understands that his resolve has vanished, that he will never find the courage to go through with it.

How much time has passed by then? Four days—no, five days—which means that only forty-eight hours are left. Brick has yet to stir from his apartment and venture outside. He has canceled all his Great Zavello performances for the week, claiming to be down with the flu, and has unplugged the phone from the wall. He suspects that Flora has been trying to reach him, but he can't bring himself to talk to her just now, knowing that the sound of her voice would upset him so much that he might lose control and start babbling inanities to her or, worse, start crying, which would only deepen her alarm. Nevertheless, on the morning of May 27, he finally shaves, showers, and puts on a fresh set of clothes. Sunlight is pouring through the windows, the beckoning radiance of the New York spring, and he decides that a walk in the air might do him some good. If his mind has failed to solve his problems for him, perhaps he will find the answer in his feet.

The instant he steps onto the sidewalk, however, he hears someone calling his name. It's a woman's voice, and because no other pedestrians are passing by at that moment, Brick is at a loss to identify where the voice is coming from. He looks around, the voice calls to him again, and behold, there is Virginia Blaine, sitting behind the wheel of a car parked directly across the street. In spite of himself, Brick is inordinately glad to see her, but as he steps down from the curb and walks over to the woman who has haunted him for the past month, a wave of apprehension flutters through him. By the time he reaches the white Mercedes sedan, he can feel his pulse pounding inside his head.

Good morning, Owen, Virginia says. Do you have a minute?

I wasn't expecting to see you again, Brick replies, looking closely at her beautiful face, which is even more beautiful than he remembered, and her dark brown hair, which is shorter than it was the last time he saw her, and her delicate mouth with the red lipstick, and her blue eyes with the long lashes, and her thin, graceful hands resting on the wheel of the car.

I hope I'm not interrupting anything, she says.

Not at all. I was just going out for a walk.

Good. Let's make it a drive instead, okay?

Where to?

I'll tell you later. We have a lot to talk about first. By the time we get to where we're going, you'll understand why I took you there.

Brick hesitates, still uncertain whether Virginia can be trusted or not, but then he realizes that he doesn't care, that in all probability he's a dead man no matter what he does. If these are the last hours of his life, he thinks, then better to spend them with her than to wait it out alone.

So off they go into the brilliant May morning, leaving New York behind them and traveling along the southern rim of Connecticut on I-95, then veering onto 395 just before New London and heading north at seventy miles an hour. Brick pays little attention to the passing landscape, choosing instead to keep his eyes on Virginia, who is wearing a pale blue cashmere sweater and a pair of white linen slacks, sitting in her brown leather seat with an air of such confidence and self-sufficiency that he is reminded of her younger self, the one that used to leave him stammering whenever he tried to talk to her. Things are different now, he tells himself. He grew up, and he isn't intimidated by her anymore. He's a bit wary, perhaps, but not of Virginia the woman—rather, of the *little cog in the big machine,* the person in cahoots with Frisk.

You're looking a lot better, Owen, she begins. No more cuts, no more bandages. And I see you've had your tooth fixed. The miracles of dentistry, huh? From beat-up boxer to Mr. Handsome again.

The subject doesn't interest Brick, and instead of making small talk about the condition of his face, he comes right to the point. Did Frisk give you the injection? he asks.

It doesn't matter how I got here, she says. The important thing is why I came.

To finish me off, I suppose.

You're wrong. I came because I was feeling guilty. I got you into this mess, and now I want to try to get you out of it.

But you're Frisk's girl. If you work for him, then you're a part of it, too.

But I don't work for him. That's only a cover.

What does that mean?

Do I have to spell it out?

You're a double agent?

Sort of.

You're not going to tell me you're with the Federals.

Of course not. I hate those murdering bastards.

Then who is it?

Patience, Owen. You have to give me some time. First things first, okay?

All right. I'm listening.

Yes, I was the one who suggested you for the job. But I didn't know what it was. Something big, they said, something vital to the outcome of the war, but they never gave me any

details. I wasn't told until you were already on the other side.
I swear, I had no idea they were going to order you to kill
someone. And then, even after I found out, I had no idea Frisk
was going to threaten to kill you if you didn't carry out the job.
I only learned about that last night. That's why I came. Because I wanted to help.

I don't believe a word you're saying.

Why should you? If I were in your place, I wouldn't believe
me either. But it's the truth.

The funny thing is, Virginia, it doesn't bother me anymore. When you lie, I mean. I like you too much to get
worked up about it. You might be a fake, you might even be
the person who winds up killing me, but I'll never stop lik-
ing you.

I like you, too, Owen.

You're a strange person. Did anyone ever tell you that?

All the time. Ever since I was a little girl.

How long has it been since you've been back on this side?

Fifteen years. This is my first trip. It wasn't even possible
until about three months ago. You were the first one to go back
and forth. Did you know that?

No one ever told me anything.

It's like stepping into a dream, isn't it? The same place, but
entirely different. America without war. It's hard to digest. You
get so used to the fighting, it kind of creeps into your bones,
and after a while, you can't imagine a world without it.

America's at war, all right. We're just not fighting it here.
Not yet, anyway.

How's your wife, Owen? It's stupid of me, but I can't remember her name.

Flora.

That's right, Flora. Do you want to call and let her know you'll be gone for a couple of days?

She isn't in New York. I sent her back to her mother in Argentina.

Smart thinking. You did the right thing.

She's pregnant, by the way. I thought you'd like to know that.

Good work, kid. Congratulations.

Flora's pregnant, I love her more than ever, I'd rather cut off my right arm than do anything to hurt her, and still, the only thing I really want right now is to go to bed with you. Does that make any sense?

Absolutely.

One last roll in the hay.

Don't talk like that. You're not going to die, Owen.

Well, what do you think? Does the idea appeal to you?

Do you remember what I said the last time you saw me?

How could I forget?

Then you already have your answer, don't you?

They cross the border into Massachusetts, and a few minutes later they stop to fill the tank with gas, visit the ladies' and men's, and eat a pair of wretched, microwaved hot dogs on soggy buns, which they wash down with gulps of bottled water. As they walk back to the car, Brick takes Virginia in his arms and kisses her, driving his tongue deep into her mouth. It is a delicious moment for him, fulfilling the dream of half a lifetime, but one also marked by shame and regret, for this small prelude to further pleasures with his old love is the first time he has touched another woman since marrying Flora. But Brick, who is nothing less than a soldier now, a man engaged in fighting a war, justifies his infidelity by reminding himself that he could well be dead by tomorrow.

Once they hit the highway again, he turns to Virginia and asks her the question he's been putting off for more than two hours: where are they going?

Two places, she says. The first one today, the next one tomorrow.

Well, that's a start, I guess. You wouldn't care to be a little more specific, would you?

I can't tell you about the first stop, because I want that to be a surprise. But tomorrow we're going to Vermont.

Vermont . . . That means Brill. You're taking me to Brill.

You catch on fast, Owen.

It won't do any good, Virginia. I've thought about going there a dozen times, but I have no idea what to say to him.

Just ask him to stop.

He'll never listen to me.

How do you know unless you try?

Because I do, that's all.

You're forgetting that I'll be with you.

What difference does that make?

I've already told you that I don't really work for Frisk. Who do you think I take my orders from?

How should I know?

Come on, Corporal. Think.

Not Brill.

Yes, Brill.

That's impossible. He's on this side, and you're on the other side. There's no way for you to communicate.

Did you ever hear of a telephone?

The phones don't work. I already tried to call when I was in Wellington. I dialed my apartment in Queens, and they said the number was out of service.

There are phones and there are phones, my friend. Given his part in all this, do you think Brill would have one that didn't work?

So you talk to him.

Constantly.

But you've never met.

No. Tomorrow is the big day.

And what about now? Why not go to him now?

Because the appointment is for tomorrow. And until then, you and I have other plans.

Your surprise . . .

Exactly.

How much longer to go?

Less than half an hour. In about two minutes, I'm going to ask you to close your eyes. You can open them again after we get there.

Brick plays along with the game, gladly submitting to Virginia's puerile whims, and for the last minutes of the journey he sits in his seat without saying a word, trying to guess what prank she has in store for him. If he were better versed in geography, he might have found a solution long before their arrival, but Brick has no more than a fuzzy understanding of maps, and since he has never actually set foot in Worcester, Massachusetts (having imagined himself there only in a dream), when the car stops and Virginia tells him to open his eyes, he is convinced he's back in Wellington. The car has pulled up in front of the suburban house they entered last month, the same brick-and-stucco manor with the luxuriant front lawn, the flower beds, and the tall, blooming bushes. When he glances down the street, however, all the neighboring houses are intact. No charred walls, no collapsed roofs, no broken windows. The war has not touched the block, and as Brick slowly turns around in a circle, trying to absorb the familiar but altered setting, the illusion finally bursts, and he knows where he is. Not Wellington but Worcester, the former name of the city in the other world.

Isn't it wonderful? Virginia says, raising her arms and gesturing to the undamaged houses. Her eyes have lit up, and a smile is spreading across her face. This is the way it used to be, Owen. Before the guns . . . before the attacks . . . before Brill started tearing everything apart. I never thought I'd live to see it again.

Let Virginia Blaine have her brief moment of joy. Let Owen Brick forget his little Flora and find comfort in the arms of Virginia Blaine. Let the man and the woman who met as children take mutual pleasure in their adult bodies. Let them

climb into bed together and do what they will. Let them eat.
Let them drink. Let them return to the bed and do what they
will to every inch and orifice of their grown-up bodies. Life
goes on, after all, even under the most painful circumstances,
goes on until the end, and then it stops. And these lives will
stop, since they must stop, since neither one of them can ever
make it to Vermont to talk to Brill, for Brill might weaken then
and give up, and Brill can never give up, since he must go on
telling his story, the story of the war in that other world, which
is also this world, and he can't allow anyone or anything to
stop him.

It's the middle of the night. Virginia is lying under the covers asleep, her sated flesh expanding and contracting as the
cool air enters and exits her lungs, dreaming God knows what
in the dim moonlight that filters through the half-open window.
Brick is on his side, his body curled around hers, one hand
cupping her left breast, the other hand poised on the rounded
area where her hip and buttock merge, but the corporal is restless, unaccountably wakeful, and after struggling to fall asleep
for close to an hour, he slips out of bed to go downstairs and
pour himself a drink, wondering if a shot of whiskey might not
quell the tremors that are rising within him as he contemplates
tomorrow's meeting with the old man. Dressed in the dead
husband's terry-cloth robe, he walks into the kitchen and
turns on the light. Confronted by the dazzle of that elegant
space, with its sleek surfaces and costly appliances, Brick begins to think about Virginia's marriage. Her husband must
have been a good deal older than she was, he muses, a sharp

operator with the wherewithal to afford a house like this one, and because Virginia has yet to say a word about him (except to mention that he was rich), the not-so-well-off magician from Queens asks himself if she cared about her departed spouse or simply married him for his money. The idle thoughts of an insomniac, searching the cupboards for a clean glass and a bottle of scotch: the endless banalities that flit through the mind as one notion mutates into the next. So it goes with all of us, young and old, rich and poor, and then an unexpected event comes crashing down on us to jolt us out of our torpor.

Brick hears the low-flying planes in the distance, then the noise of a helicopter engine, and an instant after that, the keening blast of an explosion. The windows in the kitchen shatter to bits, the floor shakes under his bare feet and then begins to tilt, as if the entire foundation of the house were shifting position, and when Brick runs into the front hall to mount the stairs and check on Virginia, he is met by large, writhing spears of flame. Wooden shards and slate roof tiles are falling down from above. Brick turns his eyes upward, and after several seconds of confusion he understands that he is looking at the night sky through clouds of billowing smoke. The top half of the house is gone, which means that Virginia is also gone, and while he knows it will serve no purpose, he desperately wants to mount the stairs and look for her body. But the stairs are on fire now, and he will burn to death if he gets any closer.

He runs outside onto the lawn, and all around him howling neighbors are pouring from their houses into the night. A contingent of Federal troops has massed in the middle of the street, fifty or sixty helmeted men, all of them armed with machine guns. Brick raises his hands in a gesture of surrender, but it doesn't do him any good. The first bullet hits him in the leg, and he falls down, clutching the wound as blood spurts onto his fingers. Before he can inspect the damage and see how badly he is hurt, a second bullet goes straight through his right eye and out the back of his head. And that is the end of Owen Brick, who leaves the world in silence, with no chance to say a last word or think a last thought.

Meanwhile, seventy-five miles to the northwest, in a white wooden house in southern Vermont, August Brill is awake, lying in bed and staring into the dark. And the war goes on.

Does it have to end that way? Yes, probably yes, although it wouldn't be difficult to think of a less brutal outcome. But what would be the point? My subject tonight is war, and now that war has entered this house, I feel I would be insulting Titus and Katya if I softened the blow. Peace on earth, good will toward men. Piss on earth, good will toward none. This is the heart of it, the black center of the dead of night, a good four hours still to burn and all hope for sleep utterly smashed. The only solution is to leave Brick behind me, make sure that he gets a decent burial, and then come up with another story. Something low to the ground this time, a counterweight to the fantastical machine I've just built. Giordano Bruno and the theory of infinite worlds. Provocative stuff, yes, but there are other stones to be unearthed as well.

War stories. Let your guard down for a moment, and they come rushing in on you, one by one by one . . .

The last time Sonia and I went to Europe together, we wound up in Brussels for a couple of days to attend a reunion of some distant branch of her family. One afternoon, we had lunch with a second cousin of hers, an old gent pushing eighty, a former publisher who had grown up in Belgium and later moved to France, an affable, well-read person who spoke in complex, highly articulated paragraphs, a walking book in the shape of a man. The restaurant was in a narrow arcade somewhere in the center of the city, and before we went inside to have our meal, he took us to a small courtyard at the end of the walkway to show us a fountain and a bronze statue of a water nymph sitting in the pool. It wasn't an especially brilliant work—a somewhat smaller than life-size rendering of a nude girl in her mid- to late teens—but in spite of its clumsiness, there were touching qualities about it as well, something about the curve of the girl's back, I think, or else the tininess of her breasts and her slender hips, or else simply the smallish scale of the piece in general. As we stood there examining it, Jean-Luc told us that the model had grown up to become his high school literature teacher and was only seventeen when she posed for the artist. We turned around and went into the restaurant, and over lunch he told us more about his connection to that woman. She was the one who made him fall in love with books, he said, because when he was her student he developed an intense crush on her, and that love wound up changing the direction of his life. When the Germans occupied Belgium in 1940, Jean-Luc was just fifteen, but he joined an underground resistance cell as a courier, attending school by day and running messages at night. His teacher joined the resistance as well, and one morning in 1942 the Germans marched into the lycée and arrested her. Shortly after that, Jean-Luc's cell was infiltrated and destroyed. He had to go into hiding, he said, and for the last eighteen months of the war he lived alone in an attic and did nothing but read books—all books, every book, from the ancient Greeks to the Renaissance to the twentieth century, consuming novels and plays, poetry and philosophy, understanding that he never could have done this without the influence of his teacher, who had been arrested before his eyes and for whom he prayed every night. When the war finally ended, he learned that she hadn't made it home from the camp, but no one could tell him how or when she had died. She had been blotted out, expunged from the face of the earth, and not a single person knew what had happened to her.

Some years after that (late forties? early fifties?), he was eating alone in a restaurant in Brussels and overheard two men talking at the next table. One of them had spent time in

a concentration camp during the war, and as he told the other
man a story about one of his fellow inmates, Jean-Luc became
more and more convinced that he was referring to his teacher,
the little water nymph sitting in the fountain at the end of the
arcade. All the details seemed to fit: a Belgian girl in her twenties, red hair, small body, extremely beautiful, a left-wing trou-
blemaker who had defied an order from one of the camp
guards. To set an example for the other prisoners and demonstrate what happens to people who disobey the guards, the
commandant decided to execute her in public, with the entire
population of the camp on hand to witness the killing. Jean-
Luc was expecting the man to say that they hanged her or
stood her up against a wall and shot her, but it turned out that
the commandant had something more traditional in mind, a
method that had gone out of fashion several centuries earlier.
Jean-Luc couldn't look at us when he spoke the words. He
turned his head away and looked out the window, as if the execution were taking place just outside the restaurant, and in a
quiet voice suddenly filled with emotion, he said: She was
drawn and quartered. With long chains attached to both her
wrists and both her ankles, she was led into the yard, made to
stand at attention as the chains were attached to four jeeps
pointing in four different directions, and then the commandant
gave the order for the drivers to start their engines. According
to the man at the next table, the woman didn't cry out, didn't
make a sound as one limb after another was pulled off her body.
Is such a thing possible? Jean-Luc was tempted to talk to the
man, he said, but then he realized that he wasn't capable of

talking. Fighting back tears, he stood up, tossed some money on the table, and left the restaurant.

Sonia and I returned to Paris, and within forty-eight hours I heard two more stories that hit me hard—not with the sickening violence of Jean-Luc's story, but hard enough to have left an enduring impact. The first one came from Alec Foyle, a British journalist who flew in from London to have dinner with us one night. Alec is in his late forties, a onetime boyfriend of Miriam's, and even if it's all water under the bridge now, Sonia and I were both a little surprised when our daughter chose Richard over him. We had been out of contact for a number of years, and there was a lot of catching up to do, which led to one of those hectic conversations that careen abruptly from one subject to the next. At a certain point we started talking about families, and Alec told us about a recent conversation he'd had with a friend, a woman who covered the arts for the *Independent* or the *Guardian*, I forget which. He said to her: At one time or another, every family lives through extraordinary events— horrendous crimes, floods and earthquakes, bizarre accidents, miraculous strokes of luck, and there isn't a family in the world without secrets and skeletons, trunkfuls of hidden material that would make your jaw drop if the lid were ever opened. His friend disagreed with him. It's true for many families, she said, maybe for most families, but not all. Her family, for example. She couldn't think of a single interesting thing that had ever happened to any of them, not one exceptional event.

Impossible, Alec said. Just concentrate for a moment, and you're bound to come up with something. So his friend thought for a while, and eventually she said: Well, maybe there's one thing. My grandmother told it to me not long before she died, and I suppose it's fairly unusual.

Alec smiled at us from across the table. Unusual, he said. My friend wouldn't have been born if this thing hadn't happened, and she called it *unusual*. As far as I'm concerned, it's bloody astonishing.

His friend's grandmother was born in Berlin in the early twenties, and when the Nazis took power in 1933, her Jewish family reacted in the same way so many others did: they believed that Hitler was nothing more than a passing upstart and made no effort to leave Germany. Even as conditions worsened, they went on hoping for the best and refused to budge. One day, when the grandmother was seventeen or eighteen, her parents received a letter signed by someone claiming to be a captain in the SS. Alec didn't mention what year it was, but 1938 would be a reasonable assumption, I think, perhaps a little earlier. According to Alec's friend, the letter read as follows: You don't know me, but I am well aware of you and your children. I could be court-martialed for writing this, but I feel it is my duty to warn you that you are in great danger. If you don't act soon, you will all be arrested and sent to a camp. Trust me, this is not idle speculation. I am willing to furnish you with exit visas that will allow you to escape to another country, but in exchange for my help, you must do me one important favor. I have fallen in love with your daughter. I have been watching her for some time now, and although we have never spoken, this love is unconditional. She is the person I have dreamed of all my life, and if this were a different world and we were ruled by different laws, I would propose marriage tomorrow. This is all I am asking: next Wednesday, at ten o'clock in the morning, your daughter will go to the park across the street from your house, sit down on her favorite bench, and stay there for two hours. I promise not to touch her, not to approach her, not to address a single word to her. I will remain hidden for the full two hours. At noon, she can stand up and return to your house. The reason for this request is no doubt evident to you by now. I need to see my darling girl one last time before I lose her forever . . .

It goes without saying that she did it. She had to do it, even though the family feared it was a hoax, not to mention the more dire possibilities of molestation, abduction, and rape. Alec's friend's grandmother was an inexperienced girl, and the fact that she had been turned into an adored Beatrice by some unknown Dante from the SS, that a stranger had been spying on her for the past several months, listening in on her conversations and following her around the city, threw her into an ever-mounting panic as she waited for Wednesday to come. Nevertheless, when the appointed hour arrived she did what she had to do and marched off to the park with her yellow star wrapped around the sleeve of her sweater, sat down on a bench, and opened the book she had carried along as a prop to still her nerves. For two straight hours, she didn't look up once. She was that scared, she told her granddaughter, and pretending to read was her only defense, the only thing that kept her from jumping up and running away. Impossible to calculate how long those two hours must have felt to her, but noon crept around at last, and she went home. The next day, the exit visas were slipped under the door as promised, and the family left for England.

The last story came from one of Sonia's nephews, the oldest son of the oldest of her three older brothers, Bertrand, the only other member of her family who had become a musician, and therefore someone special to her, a violinist in the orchestra of the Paris Opera, a colleague and a pal. The afternoon following our dinner with Alec, we met him for lunch at Allard, and midway through the meal he started talking about a cellist in the orchestra who was planning to retire at the end of the season. Everyone knew her story, he said, she talked about it openly, and so he didn't feel he would be breaking any confidence if he told it to us. Françoise Duclos. I have no idea why her name is still with me, but there it is—Françoise Duclos, the cellist. She married her husband in the mid-sixties, Bertrand said, gave birth to a daughter in the early seventies, and two years after that the husband vanished. Not such an uncommon occurrence, as the police told her when she reported him missing, but Françoise knew that her husband loved her, that he was crazy about their little girl, and, unless she was the blindest, most obtuse woman on earth, that he wasn't involved with another woman. He earned a decent salary, which meant that money wasn't an issue, he enjoyed his work, and he had never shown any penchant for gambling or risky investments. So what happened to him, and why did he disappear? No one knew.

Fifteen years went by. The husband was declared legally dead, but Françoise never remarried or lived with another man. She raised her daughter on her own (with help from her parents), was hired by the orchestra, gave private lessons in her apartment, and that was it: a pared-down existence, with a handful of friends, summers in the country with her brother's family, and an unsolved mystery as her constant companion. Then, after all those years of silence, the telephone rang one day, and she was asked to go to the morgue to identify a body. The person who accompanied her into the room where the corpse was waiting warned her that she was in for a rough experience: the deceased had been pushed from a sixth-floor window and had died on contact with the pavement. Shattered as the body was, Françoise recognized it at once. He was twenty pounds heavier than he had been, his hair was thinner and had turned gray, but there was no question that she was looking at the corpse of her missing husband.

Before she could leave, a man entered the room, took Françoise by the arm, and said: Please come with me, Madame Duclos. I have something to tell you.

He led her outside, took her to his car, which was parked in front of a bakery on an adjacent street, and asked her to climb in. Rather than put the key in the ignition, the man rolled down the window and lit up a cigarette. Then, for the next hour, he told Françoise the story of the past fifteen years as she sat next to him in his little blue car, watching people walk out of the bakery carrying loaves of bread. That was one detail Bertrand remembered—the loaves of bread—but he couldn't tell us anything about the man. His name, his age, what he looked like—all a blank, but finally that's of scant importance.

Duclos was an agent for the DGSE, he told her. She couldn't have known that, of course, since agents are under strict orders not to talk about their work, and all those years when she thought her husband was writing economic studies for the Ministry of Foreign Affairs, he was actually operating as a spy under the Direction Générale de la Sécurité Extérieure. Just after the birth of their daughter seventeen years ago, he was given an assignment that turned him into a double agent: ostensibly acting in support of the Soviets but in fact feeding information to the French. After two years, the Russians found out what he was up to and tried to kill him. Duclos managed to escape, but from that point on returning home was no longer possible. The Russians were keeping watch on Françoise and her daughter, the phone in the apartment was tapped, and if Duclos tried to call or visit, all three of them would have been murdered instantly.

So he stayed away to protect his family, hidden by the French for fifteen years as he moved from one Paris apartment to another, a hunted man, a haunted man, stealing out to catch an occasional glimpse of his daughter, watching her grow up from afar, never able to talk to her, to know her, observing his wife as her youthful looks slowly vanished and she lapsed into middle

age, and then, because of carelessness, or because someone in-
formed on him, or because of sheer dumb luck, the Russians finally caught up with Duclos. The capture . . . the blindfold . . .
the ropes around his wrists . . . the punches to his face and
body . . . and then the plunge from the sixth-floor window. Death
by defenestration. Another classic method, the execution of
choice among spies and policemen for hundreds of years.

There were numerous gaps in Bertrand's account, but he
couldn't answer any of the questions Sonia and I asked him.
How had Duclos occupied himself during all those years? Did
he live under a false name? Had he gone on working for the
DGSE in some capacity or other? How often was he able to go
out? Bertrand shook his head. He simply didn't know.

What year did Duclos die? I asked. You must remember that.

Nineteen eighty-nine. The spring of eighty-nine. I'm sure
of it, because that's when I joined the orchestra, and the thing
with Françoise happened just a few weeks later.

The spring of eighty-nine, I said. The Berlin Wall came
down in November. The Eastern bloc threw out their govern-
ments, and then the Soviet Union fell apart. That makes Duclos one of the last casualties of the Cold War, doesn't it?

I clear my throat, and a second later I'm coughing again,
retching up gobs of sputum as I cover my mouth to stifle the
noise. I want to spit into my handkerchief, but when I reach
out and search for it with my fingers, I brush against the alarm
clock, which falls off the night table and clatters onto the

floor. Still no handkerchief. Then I remember that all my handkerchiefs are in the wash, so I swallow hard and let the goo slide down my throat, telling myself for the fiftieth time in the past fifty days to stop smoking, which I know will never happen, but I say it anyway, just to torture myself with my own hypocrisy.

I start thinking about Duclos again, wondering if I might not be able to tease a story out of that awful business, not necessarily Duclos and Françoise, not the fifteen years of hiding and waiting, not what I already know, but something I can make up as I go along. The daughter, for instance, thrust forward from 1989 to 2007. What if she grows up to become a journalist or a novelist, a scribbler of some sort, and after her mother's death she decides to write a book about her parents? But the man who betrayed her father to the Russians is still alive, and when he gets wind of what she's up to, he tries to stop her—or even kill her . . .

That's as far as I get. A moment later, I hear footsteps on the second floor again, but this time they aren't heading for the bathroom, they're coming down the stairs, and as I imagine Miriam or Katya going into the kitchen to look for a drink or a cigarette or a snack from the refrigerator, I realize that the steps are coming in this direction, that someone is approaching my room. I hear a knock on the door—no, not exactly a knock, but a faint scratching of fingernails against the wood—and then Katya whispers, Are you awake?

I tell her to come in, and as the door opens I can make out her silhouette against the dim, bluish light behind her. She seems to be wearing her Red Sox T-shirt and gray sweatpants, and her long hair is tied back in a ponytail.

Are you all right? she asks. I heard something fall on the floor, and then a lot of terrible coughing.

I'm right as rain, I answer. Whatever that means.

Have you slept at all?

Not a wink. What about you?

In and out, but not much.

Why don't you close the door? It's better in here when it's completely dark. I'll give you one of my pillows, and you can lie down next to me.

The door shuts, I slide a pillow over to Sonia's old spot, and a few moments later Katya is stretched out on her back beside me.

It reminds me of when you were little, I say. When your grandmother and I came to visit, you always crawled into bed with us.

I miss her like crazy, you know. I still can't get it into my head that she isn't around anymore.

You and everyone else.

Why did you stop writing your book, Grandpa?

I decided it was more fun to watch movies with you.

That's recent. You stopped writing it a long time ago.

It got too sad. I enjoyed working on the early parts, but then I came to the bad times, and I started to struggle with it. I've done such stupid things in my life, I didn't have the heart to live through them again. Then Sonia got sick. After she died, the thought of going back to it revolted me.

You shouldn't be so hard on yourself.

I'm not. I'm just being honest.

The book was supposed to be for me, remember?

For you and your mother.

But she already knows everything. I don't. That's why I was looking forward to reading it so much.

You probably would have been bored.

You can be a real fathead sometimes, Grandpa. Did you know that?

Why do you still call me *Grandpa*? You stopped calling your mother *Mom* years ago. You must have been in high school, and suddenly *Mom* became *Mother*.

I didn't want to sound like a baby anymore.

I call you Katya. You could call me August.

I never liked that name very much. It looks good on paper, but it's hard to get it out of your mouth.

Something else, then. How about *Ed*?

Ed? Where did that come from?

I don't know, I say, doing my best to imitate a Cockney accent. It just popped into me little ole 'ed.

Katya lets out a brief, sarcastic groan.

I'm sorry, I continue. I can't help myself. I was born with the bad joke gene, and there's nothing I can do about it.

You never take anything seriously, do you?

I take everything seriously, my love. I just pretend not to.

August Brill, my grandfather, currently known as Ed. What did they call you when you were little?

Augie, mostly. On my good days I was Augie, but people called me a lot of other things, too.

It's hard to imagine it. You as a child, I mean. You must have been a weird kid. Reading books all the time, I'll bet.

That came later. Until I was fifteen, the only thing I cared about was baseball. We used to play it nonstop, all the way into November. Then it was football for a few months, but by the end of February we'd start in on baseball again. The old gang from Washington Heights. We were so nuts, we even played baseball in the snow.

What about girls? Do you remember the name of your first big love?

Of course. You never forget a thing like that.

Who was she?

Virginia Blaine. I fell for her when I was a sophomore in high school, and suddenly baseball didn't matter anymore. I started reading poetry, I took up smoking, and I fell in love with Virginia Blaine.

Did she love you back?

I was never sure. She went hot and cold on me for about six months, and then she skipped off with someone else. It felt like the end of the world, my first real heartbreak.

Then you met Grandma. You were only twenty, right? Younger than I am now.

You're asking a lot of questions . . .

If you're not going to finish your book, how else am I going to find out what I need to know?

Why the sudden interest?

It's not sudden. I've been thinking about it for a long time.

When I heard you were awake just now, I said to myself, Here's my chance, and I came down and knocked on your door.

Scratched on my door.

All right, scratched. But here we are now, lying in the dark, and if you don't answer my questions, I'm not going to let you watch movies with me anymore.

Speaking of which, I came up with another example to support your theory.

Good. But we're not talking about films now. We're talking about you.

It's not such a pleasant story, Katya. There are a lot of depressing things in it.

I'm a big girl, Ed. I can handle anything you dish out.

I wonder.

As far as I know, the only depressing thing you're talking about is the fact that you cheated on your wife and left her for another woman. I'm sorry, chum, but that's pretty standard practice around here, isn't it? You think I can't handle that? I already have, with my own father and mother.

When did you speak to him last?

Who?

Your father.

Who?

Come on, Katya. Your father, Richard Furman, your mother's ex-husband, my ex-son-in-law. Talk to me a little, sweetheart. I promise to answer your questions, but just let me know when you last heard from your father.

About two weeks ago, I guess.

Did you make any arrangements to see each other?

He invited me to come to Chicago, but I told him I wasn't feeling up to it. When the semester's over next month, he said he'd come to New York for a weekend and we could stay at a hotel somewhere and eat lots of good food. I'll probably go, but I haven't decided yet. His wife's pregnant, by the way. Pretty Suzie Woozy is with child.

Does your mother know?

I didn't tell her. I thought she might be upset.

She's bound to find out eventually.

I know. But she seems to be doing a little better now, and I didn't want to rock the boat.

You're one tough cookie, kid.

No, I'm not. I'm a big soft jelly doughnut. All ooze and mush.

I take hold of Katya's hand, and for the next half minute or so we look up into the dark without saying a word. I wonder if she might not drift off to sleep if I don't resume the conversation, but a moment after I think that thought she breaks the silence by asking me another question:

When was the first time you saw her?

April fourth, nineteen fifty-five—at two-thirty in the afternoon.

For real?

For real.

Where were you?

Broadway. Broadway and One Hundred-fifteenth Street, walking uptown on my way to Butler Library. Sonia went to

Juilliard, which was near Columbia at the time, and she was walking downtown. I must have spotted her about half a block away, probably because she was wearing a red coat—red jumps out at you, especially on a city street, with nothing but drab bricks and stones in the background. So I catch sight of the red coat coming toward me, and then I see that the person wearing the coat is a short girl with dark hair. Quite promising from a distance, but still too far away to be sure of anything. That's how it is with boys, you know that. Always looking at girls, always sizing them up, always hoping to run into the knockout beauty who will suck the breath out of you and make your heart stop beating. So I've seen the red coat, and I've seen that it's worn by a girl with short dark hair who stands approximately five feet five inches tall, and the next thing I notice is that her head is bobbing around a little bit, as if she's humming to herself, and that there's a certain bounce to her step, a lightness in the way she moves, and I say to myself, This girl is happy, happy to be alive and walking down the street in the crisp, sun-drenched air of early spring. A few seconds later, her face begins to acquire more definition, and I see that she's wearing bright red lipstick, and then, as the distance between us continues to narrow, I simultaneously absorb two important facts. One: that she is indeed humming to herself—a Mozart aria, I think, but can't be certain—and not only is she humming, she has the voice of a real singer. Two: that she's sublimely attractive, perhaps even beautiful, and that my heart is about to stop beating. By now, she's only four or five feet away, and I, who have never stopped to talk to an unknown girl on the street, who have never in my life had the audacity to address a good-looking stranger in public, open my mouth and say hello, and because I'm smiling at her, no doubt smiling in a way that carries no threat or hint of aggression, she stops humming, smiles back at me, and returns my greeting with one of her own. And that's it. I'm too nervous to say anything more, and so I keep on walking, as does the pretty girl in the red coat, but after six or seven steps I regret my lack of boldness and turn around, hoping there's still time to initiate a conversation, but the girl is walking too quickly and is already out of range, and so, with my eyes on her back, I watch her cross the street and disappear into the crowd.

Frustrating—but understandable. I hate it when men try to pick me up on the street. If you'd acted more boldly, Sonia probably would have been turned off, and you wouldn't have gotten anywhere with her.

That's a generous way of looking at it. After she disappeared, I felt I'd blown the opportunity of a lifetime.

How long did it take before you saw her again?

Almost a month. The days dragged on, and I couldn't stop thinking about her. If I had known she was a student at Juilliard, I might have been able to track her down, but I didn't know anything. She was just a beautiful apparition who had looked into my eyes for a couple of seconds and then vanished. I was convinced I would never see her again. The gods had tricked me, and the girl I was destined to fall in love with, the one person who had been put on this earth to give my life meaning, had been snatched away and thrown into another dimension—an inaccessible place, a place I would never be allowed to enter. I remember writing a long, ridiculous poem about parallel worlds, lost chances, the tragic shittiness of fate. Twenty years old, and already I felt cursed.

But fate was on your side.

Fate, luck, whatever you want to call it.

Where did it happen?

On the subway. The Seventh Avenue IRT. Heading downtown on the evening on April twenty-seventh, nineteen fifty-five. The car was crowded, but the seat next to mine was empty. We stopped at Sixty-sixth Street, the doors opened, and in she walked. Since there were no other seats available, she sat down beside me.

Did she remember you?

A vague recollection. I reminded her of our little encounter on Broadway earlier that month, and then it came back to her. We didn't have much time. I was on my way to the Village to meet some friends, but Sonia was getting off at Forty-second Street, so we were together for only three stops. We managed to introduce ourselves and exchange phone numbers. I learned that she was studying at Juilliard. I learned that she was French but had spent the first twelve years of her life in America. Her English was perfect, no accent at all. When I tried out some of my mediocre French on her, her French turned out to be perfect as well. We probably talked for seven minutes, ten minutes at the most. Then she got off, and I knew that something monumental had happened. For me, in any case. I couldn't know what Sonia was thinking or feeling, but after those seven or ten minutes, I knew that I had met the one.

First date. First kiss. First . . . you know what.

I called her the next afternoon. Trembling hands . . . I must
have picked up the receiver and put it down three or four
times before I found the courage to dial. An Italian restaurant
in the West Village, I can't remember the name anymore. Inex-
pensive, I didn't have much money, and this was the first
time—it's hard to believe—the first time I'd ever asked a girl
out to *dinner*. I can't see myself. I have no idea what kind of
impression I made, but I can see her sitting across from me in
her white blouse, her steady green eyes, watchful, alert,
amused, and that superb mouth with the rounded lips, smiling,
smiling often, and her low voice, a resonant voice that came
from somewhere deep in her diaphragm, an extremely sexy
voice, I found, always did, and then her laugh, which was
much higher, almost squeaky at times, a laugh that seemed to
emerge from her throat, even her head, and whenever something tickled her funny bone—I'm talking about later now, not
that night—she would go into these wild giggling fits, laughing
so hard that tears would come streaming from her eyes.

I remember. I never saw anyone laugh like her. When I was
little, I sometimes got scared by it. She would go on for so long,
I thought it would never stop, that she would actually die
laughing. Then I grew to love it.

So there we were, two twenty-year-old kids in that restaurant on Bank Street, Perry Street, wherever it was, out on our
first date. We talked about a lot of things, most of which I've forgotten, but I remember how taken I was when she told me about
her family, her background. My own story seemed so dull by

comparison, with my furniture-salesman father and fourth-grade schoolteacher mother, the Brills of upper Manhattan, who had never gone anywhere or done anything but work and pay the rent. Sonia's father was a research biologist, a professor, one of the top scientists in Europe. Alexandre Weil—a distant relative of the composer—born in Strasbourg, a Jew (as you already know), and therefore what a fortunate turn when Princeton offered him a job in 1935 and he had the good sense to accept it. If the family had stayed in France during the war, who knows what would have happened to them? Sonia's mother, Marie-Claude, was born in Lyon. I forget what her father did, but both of her grandfathers were Protestant ministers, which means that Sonia was hardly your typical French girl. No Catholics anywhere in sight, no Hail Marys, no visits to the confession box. Marie-Claude met Alexandre when they were students in Paris, and the marriage took place sometime in the early twenties. Four kids in all: three boys and then, five years after the last one was born, along came Sonia, the baby of the bunch, the little princess, who was only one month old when the family left for America. They didn't go back to Paris until nineteen forty-seven. Alexandre was given an important position at the Pasteur Institute—*directeur* was his title, I think—and Sonia wound up going to the Lycée Fénelon. She had already made up her mind to become a singer and didn't want to finish her *bac*, but her parents insisted. That's why she went to Juilliard instead of the conservatory in Paris. She was pissed off at her parents for bearing down on her so hard and more or less ran away. But all was forgiven in the end, and by the time

I met Sonia, peace had broken out among the Weils. The family welcomed me in. I think they were touched by the fact that I came from a mixed family, too—in my case a Jewish mother and an Episcopalian father—and so, according to some mystical, unwritten code about clans and tribal loyalties, they figured that Sonia and I would be a good match.

You're getting ahead of yourself. Go back to nineteen fifty-five. The first kiss. The moment when you realized that Sonia cared about you.

A clear memory, because physical contact occurred that same night, in front of the door of her apartment. She shared a place on One Hundred-fourteenth Street with two other girls from Juilliard, and after riding back uptown on the subway, I walked her to her building. Two short blocks, from One Hundred-sixteenth to One Hundred-fourteenth, but during that brief trajectory, very close to the beginning, with perhaps the tenth or twelfth step we took, your grandmother slipped her arm around mine, and the thrill of that moment has lingered in your grandfather's heart to this day. Sonia made the first move. There was nothing overtly erotic about it—merely a silent declaration that she liked me, that she had enjoyed our evening together, and that she had every intention of seeing me again— but that gesture meant so much . . . and made me so happy, I nearly fell to the ground. Then the door. Saying good night at the door, the classic scene of every budding courtship. To kiss or not to kiss? To nod or shake hands? To brush your fingers against her cheek? To take her in your arms and hug her? So many possibilities, so little time to choose. How to read someone else's desires, how to enter the thoughts of someone you barely know? I didn't want to scare her off by acting too forward, but neither did I want her to think I was some timid soul who didn't know his own mind. The middle road, then, which I improvised as follows: I put my hands on her shoulders, leaned forward and down (down because she was shorter than I was), and pressed my lips against hers—rather hard. No tongue involved, no enveloping hug, but a good solid buss for all that. I heard a quiet rumbling in Sonia's throat, a low-pitched *m*-sound, mmmm, and then a slight catch to her breath, a drop to another register, and something that resembled a laugh. I backed away, saw that she was smiling, and put my arms around her. An instant later, her arms were around me, and then I dove in for a real kiss, a French kiss, a French kiss with the French girl who was suddenly the only person who counted anymore. Just one, but a long one, and then, not wanting to overplay my hand, I said good night and headed for the stairs.

Pas mal, mon ami.

A kiss for the ages.

Now I need a sociology lesson. We're talking about nineteen fifty-five, and from all I've heard and read, the fifties weren't the best time for young people. I'm talking about young people and sex. These days, most kids start screwing in their teens, and by the time they've hit twenty, they're old pros at it. So there you are at twenty. Your first date with Sonia has just ended with a triumphant, slobbering kiss. You clearly have the hots for each other. But the prevailing wisdom of the period says: no sex before marriage, at least if you're a girl.

You didn't get married until nineteen fifty-seven. You're not going to tell me you held back for two years, are you?

Of course not.

That's a relief.

Horniness is a human constant, the engine that drives the world, and even back then, in the dark age of the mid-twentieth century, students were fucking like rabbits.

Such language, Grandpa.

I thought you'd appreciate it.

That's just it. I do.

On the other hand, I'm not going to pretend there weren't a lot of girls who believed in the myth of the virgin bride, middle-class girls mostly, the so-called good girls, but we mustn't exaggerate either. The obstetrician who delivered your mother in nineteen sixty had been a doctor for almost twenty years. As she was stitching up Sonia's episiotomy after Miriam was born, she assured me that she was going to do a terrific job. She was an expert with the needle, she said, because she'd had so much practice: sewing up girls for their wedding nights to make the husbands think they'd married a virgin.

The things I never knew . . .

That was the fifties. Sex everywhere, but people closed their eyes and made believe it wasn't happening. In America anyway. What made things different for me and your grand-mother was the fact that she was French. There are countless hypocrisies in French life, but sex isn't one of them. Sonia moved back to Paris when she was twelve and stayed there un-til she was nineteen. Her education was far more advanced

than mine, and she was prepared to do things that would have
sent most American girls shrieking from the bed.

Such as?

Use your imagination, Katya.

You're not going to shock me, you know. I went to Sarah
Lawrence, remember? The sex capital of the Western world.
I've been all around the block, believe me.

The body has a limited number of orifices. Let's just say
that we explored every one of them.

In other words, Grandma was good in bed.

That's a blunt way of putting it, but yes, she was good. Un-
inhibited, comfortable in her body, sensitive to the shifts and
swerves of her own feelings. Every time we did it, it seemed to
be different from the time before. Fierce and dramatic one day,
slow and languid the next, the surprise of it all, the endless
nuances . . .

I remember her hands, the gentleness of her hands when
she touched me.

Gentle hands, yes. But strong hands, too. Wise hands.
That's how I used to think of them. Hands that could speak.

Did you live together before you were married?

No, no, that was out of the question. We had to sneak
around a lot. It had its exciting aspects, but most of the time it
was frustrating. I was still living with my parents in Washington Heights, so I didn't have a place of my own. And Sonia had
her two roommates. We'd go there whenever they were gone,
but that didn't happen often enough to satisfy us.

What about hotels?

Off-limits. Even if we could have afforded them, it was too dangerous. There were laws in New York that made it illegal for unmarried couples to be alone together in the same room. Every hotel had a detective—the house dick—and if he caught you, you'd be thrown in jail.

Lovely.

So what to do? Sonia had lived in Princeton as a child, and she still had friends there. There was one couple—the Gontorskis, I'll never forget them—a physics professor and his wife, refugees from Poland who loved Sonia and didn't give a damn about American sexual customs. They let us stay in their guest room on the weekends. And then there was the outdoor sex, the warm-weather sex in fields and meadows outside the city. A large element of risk. Someone finally found us naked in the bushes, and we got cold feet after that and stopped taking chances. Without the Gontorskis, we would have been in hell.

Why didn't you just get married? Right then, while you were still students.

The draft. The minute I graduated from college, I was going to be called up for my physical, and we figured I'd have to spend two years in the army. Sonia was already singing professionally by my senior year, and what if they shipped me off to West Germany or Greenland or South Korea? I couldn't have asked her to follow me. It wouldn't have been fair.

But you never were in the army, were you? Not if you were married in nineteen fifty-seven.

I flunked the exam. A false diagnosis, as it turned out—but no matter, I was free, and a month later we were married. We didn't have much money, of course, but the situation wasn't quite desperate. Sonia had dropped out of Juilliard and started her career, and by the time I left college I had already published about a dozen articles and reviews. We sublet a railroad flat in Chelsea, sweated out one New York summer, and then Sonia's oldest brother, Patrice, a civil engineer, was hired to build a dam somewhere in Africa and offered us his Paris apartment rent-free. We jumped. The minute his telegram arrived, we started packing our bags.

I'm not interested in real estate, and I already know about your careers. I want you to tell me about the important things. What was she like? How did it feel being married to her? How well did you get along? Did you ever fight? The nuts and bolts, Grandpa, not just a string of superficial facts.

All right, let me change gears and think for a moment. What was Sonia like? What did I discover about her after we were married that I hadn't known before? Contradictions. Complexities. A darkness that revealed itself slowly over time and made me reassess who she was. I loved her madly, Katya, you have to understand that, and I'm not criticizing her for being who she was. It's just that as I got to know her better, I came to realize how much suffering she carried around inside her. In most ways, your grandmother was an extraordinary person. Tender, kind, loyal, forgiving, full of spirit, with a tremendous capacity for love. But she would drift off every now and then, sometimes right in the middle of a conversation, and start staring into space with this dreamy expression in her eyes, and it was as if she didn't know me anymore. At first, I imagined she was

thinking some profound thought or remembering something
that had happened to her, but when I finally asked her what was
going through her head at those moments, she smiled at me and
said, Nothing. It was as if her whole being would empty out,
and she'd lose contact with herself and the world. All her in-
stincts and impulses about other people were deep, uncannily
deep, but her relation to herself was strangely shallow. She had
a good mind, but essentially she was uneducated, and she had
trouble following a train of thought, couldn't concentrate on
anything for very long. Except her music, which was the most
important thing in her life. She believed in her talent, but at the
same time she knew her limits and refused to tackle pieces she
felt were beyond her ability to perform well. I admired her hon-
esty, but there was also something sad about it, as if she thought
of herself as second-rate, doomed always to be a notch or two
below the best. That's why she never did any opera. Lieder, en-
semble work in choral pieces, undemanding solo cantatas—
but she never pushed herself beyond that. Did we fight? Of
course we fought. All couples fight, but she was never vicious
or cruel when we argued. Most of the time, I have to admit,
her criticisms of me were spot-on. For a Frenchwoman, she
turned out to be a rather lousy cook, but she liked good food,
so we ate in restaurants fairly often. An indifferent housekeeper, absolutely no interest in possessions—I say that as a
compliment—and even though she was a beautiful young
woman with an adorable body, she didn't dress very well. She
loved clothes, but she never seemed to choose the right ones.
To be frank, I sometimes felt lonely with her, lonely in my

work, since all my time was spent reading and writing about books, and she didn't read much, and what she did read she found difficult to talk about.

I'm getting the impression that you felt disappointed.

No, not disappointed. Far from it. Two newlyweds gradually adjusting to each other's foibles, the revelations of intimacy. All in all, it was a happy time for me, for both of us, with no serious complaints on either side, and then the dam in Africa was finished, and we went back to New York with Sonia three months pregnant.

Where did you live?

I thought you weren't interested in real estate.

That's right, I'm not. Question withdrawn.

Several places over the years. But when your mother was born, our apartment was on West Eighty-fourth Street, just off Riverside Drive. One of the windiest streets in the city.

What kind of baby was she?

Easy and difficult. Screaming and laughing. Great fun and a terrible pain in the ass.

In other words, a baby.

No. The baby of babies. Because she was *our* baby, and *our* baby was like no other baby in the world.

How long did Grandma wait until she went back to performing?

She took a year off from traveling, but she was singing in New York again when Miriam was just three months old. You know what a good mother she was—your own mother must have told you that a hundred times—but she also had her work.

It was what she was born to do, and I never would have dreamed of trying to hold her back. Still, she had her doubts, especially in the beginning. One day, when Miriam was about six months old, I walked into the bedroom, and there was Sonia on her knees by the bed, hands together, head raised, murmuring to herself in French. My French was quite good by then, and I understood everything she said. To my astonishment, it turned out that she was praying. Dear God, give me a sign and tell me what to do about my little girl. Dear God, fill the emptiness inside me and teach me how to love, to forbear, to give myself to others. She looked and sounded like a child, a small, simpleminded child, and I have to say that I was a little thrown by it—but also moved, deeply, deeply moved. It was as if a door had opened, and I was looking at a new Sonia, a different person from the one I'd known for the past five years. When she realized I was in the room, she turned around and gave me an embarrassed smile. I'm sorry, she said, I didn't want you to know. I walked over to the bed and sat down. Don't be sorry, I told her. I'm just a little puzzled, that's all. We had a long talk after that, at least an hour, the two of us sitting side by side on the bed, discussing the mysteries of her soul. Sonia explained that it started toward the end of her pregnancy, in the middle of the seventh month. She was walking down the street one afternoon on her way home, when all of a sudden a feeling of joy rose up inside her, an inexplicable, overwhelming joy. It was as if the entire universe were rushing into her body, she said, and in that instant she understood that everything was connected to everything else, that everyone in the world was connected to everyone else in the world, and this binding force, this power that held everything and everyone together, was God. That was the only word she could think of. God. Not a Jewish or Christian God, not the God of any religion, but God as the presence that animates all life. She started talking to him after that, she said, convinced that he could hear what she was saying, and these monologues, these prayers, these supplications—whatever you wanted to call them—always comforted her, always put her on an even keel with herself again. It had been going on for months now, but she didn't want to tell me because she was afraid I would think she was stupid. I was so much smarter than she was, so superior to her when it came to intellectual matters—her words, not mine—and she was worried that I'd burst out laughing at my ignorant wife when she told me that she'd found God. I didn't laugh. Heathen that I am, I didn't laugh. Sonia had her own way of thinking and her own way of doing things, and who was I to make fun of her?

I knew her all my life, but she never spoke to me about God, not once.

That's because she stopped believing. When our marriage broke up, she felt that God had abandoned her. That was a long time ago, angel, long before you were born.

Poor Grandma.

Yes, poor Grandma.

I have a theory about your marriage. Mother and I have talked about it, and she tends to go along with me, but I need confirmation, the inside dope from the horse's mouth. How would you respond if I said: You and Grandma got divorced because of her career?

My answer would be: Nonsense.

All right, not her career per se. The fact that she traveled so much.

I would say you were getting warmer—but only as an indirect cause, a secondary factor.

Mother says she used to hate it when Grandma went on tour. She'd break down and cry, she'd scream, she'd beg her not to go. Hysterical scenes . . . unadulterated anguish . . . separation after separation . . .

That happened once or twice, but I wouldn't make too big an issue of it. When Miriam was very young, say from one to six, Sonia never left for more than a week at a time. My mother would move in with us to take care of her, and things went rather smoothly. Your great-grandmother had a knack with little kids, she adored Miriam—who was her only granddaughter—and Miriam couldn't wait for her to show up. It all comes back to me now . . . the funny things your mother used to do. When she was three or four, she became fascinated by her grandmother's breasts. They were quite huge, I have to say, since my mother had grown into a fairly chunky broad by then. Sonia was small on top, with little adolescent breasts that filled out only when she was nursing Miriam, but after your mother was weaned, they got even smaller than they'd been before the pregnancy. The contrast was utterly stark, and Miriam couldn't help noticing. My mother had a voluminous chest, twenty times the size of Sonia's. One Saturday morning, she and Miriam were sitting on the sofa together watching cartoons. A commercial for pizza came on, which ended with the words: Now, that's a pizza! A moment later, your mother turned to my mother, clamped her mouth on her grandmother's right breast, and then came up shouting: Now, *that's* a pizza! My mother laughed so hard, she let out a fart, a gigantic trumpet blast of a fart. That got Miriam laughing so wildly, she peed in her pants. She jumped off the sofa and started running around the room, yelling at the top of her lungs: Fart-pee, fart-pee, *oui, oui, oui!*

You're making this up.

No, it really happened, I swear it did. The only reason I mention it is to show you that it wasn't all gloom in the house when Sonia was gone. Miriam didn't mope around feeling like some neglected Oliver Twist. She was mostly fine.

And what about you?

I learned to live with it.

That sounds like an evasive answer.

There were different periods, different stages, and each one had its own texture. In the beginning, Sonia was relatively un-known. She'd done a little singing in New York before we moved to Paris, but she had to start all over again in France, and then, just when things seemed to be taking off a bit, we came back to America, and she had to make another start. In the end, it all worked to her advantage, since she was known both here and in Europe. But it took time for her to develop a reputation. The turning point came in sixty-seven or sixty-eight, when she signed the contract to make those records with Nonesuch, but until then she didn't go away that often. I was torn down the middle. On the one hand, I was happy for her whenever she got a booking to perform in a new city. On the other hand—just like your mother—I hated to see her go. The only choice was to learn to live with it. That's not an evasion, it's a fact.

You were faithful . . .

Totally.

And when did you start to slip?

Stray is probably the word to use in this context.

Or *lapse*. There's a spiritual connotation to it that seems fitting.

All right, lapse. Around nineteen seventy, I suppose. But there was nothing spiritual about it. It was all about sex, sex pure and simple. Summer came, and Sonia went off on a three-month tour of Europe—with your mother, by the way—and there I was by myself, still just thirty-five years old, hormones roaring at full tilt, womanless in New York. I worked hard every day, but the nights were empty, colorless, stagnant. I began hanging out with a bunch of sportswriters, most of them heavy drinkers, playing poker until three in the morning, going out to bars, not because I especially liked any of them, but it was something to do, and I needed a little company after being alone all day. One night, after another boozy session in a bar, I was walking home from midtown to the Upper West Side, and I spotted a prostitute standing in the doorway of a building. A very attractive girl, as it happened, and I was drunk enough to accept her offer of a good time. Am I upsetting you?

A little.

I wasn't planning to give you any details. Just the general drift.

That's okay. It's my fault. I've turned this into Truth Night at Castle Despair, and now that we've started, we might as well go all the way.

Onward, then?

Yes, keep telling the story.

So I had my good time, which wasn't a good time at all, but after fifteen years of sleeping with the same woman I found it fascinating to touch another body, to feel flesh that was different from the flesh I knew. That was the discovery of that night. The novelty of being with another woman.

Did you feel guilty?

No. I considered it an experiment. A lesson learned, so to speak.

So my theory is right. If Grandma had been home in New York, you never would have paid that girl to sleep with you.

In that particular case, yes. But there was more to our downfall than infidelity, more to it than Sonia's absences. I've thought about this for years, and the only half-reasonable explanation I've ever come up with is that there's something wrong with me, a flaw in the mechanism, a damaged part gumming up the works. I'm not talking about moral weakness. I'm talking about my mind, my mental makeup. I'm somewhat better now, I think, the problem seemed to diminish as I grew older, but back then, at thirty-five, thirty-eight, forty, I walked around with a feeling that my life had never truly belonged to me, that I had never truly inhabited myself, that I had never been real. And because I wasn't real, I didn't understand the effect I had on others, the damage I could cause, the hurt I could inflict on the people who loved me. Sonia was my ground, my one solid connection to the world. Being with her made me better than I actually was—healthier, stronger, saner—and because we started living together when we were so young, the flaw was masked for all those years, and I assumed I was just like everyone else. But I wasn't. The moment I began to wander away from her, the bandage dropped off my wound, and then the bleeding wouldn't stop. I went after other women because I felt I'd missed out on something and had to make up for lost time. I'm talking about sex now, nothing but sex, but you can't run around and act the way I did and expect your marriage to hold together. I deceived myself into thinking it would.

Don't hate yourself so much, Grandpa. She took you back, remember?

I know . . . but all those wasted years. It makes me sick to think about them. My dumb-ass flings and dalliances. What did they add up to? A few cheap thrills, nothing of any importance—but there's no question that they laid the groundwork for what happened next.

Oona McNally.

Sonia was so trusting, and I was so discreet, our life went on together without any crucial disturbances. She didn't know, and I didn't tell, and not for one second did I ever think of leaving her. Then, in nineteen seventy-four, I wrote a favorable review of a first novel by a young American author. *Anticipation,* by the aforementioned O.M. It was a startling book, I felt, highly original and written with great command, a strong, promising debut. I didn't know anything about the writer—only that she was twenty-six years old and lived in New York. I read the book in galleys, and since galleys didn't have author photos on them in the seventies, I didn't even know what she looked like. About four months later, I went to a poetry reading at the Gotham Book Mart (without Sonia, who was at home with Miriam), and when the reading was over and we all started walking down the stairs, someone grabbed me by the arm. Oona McNally. She wanted to thank me for the nice review I'd given her novel. That was the extent of it, but I was so impressed by her looks—tall and lithe, an exquisite face, the second coming of Virginia Blaine—that I asked her out for a drink. How many times had I betrayed Sonia by then? Three or four one-night stands, and one mini-affair that lasted roughly two weeks. Not such a gruesome catalogue when compared to some men, but enough to have taught me that I was prepared to seize opportunities whenever they presented themselves. But this girl was different. You didn't sleep with Oona McNally and say good-bye to her the next morning—you fell in love with her, you wanted her to be part of your life. I won't bore you with the tawdry incidentals. The clandestine dinners, the long talks in out-of-the-way bars, the slow mutual seduction. She didn't jump into my arms immediately. I had to go after her, win her confidence, persuade her that it was possible for a man to be in love with two women at the same time. I still had no intention of leaving Sonia, you understand. I wanted both of them. My wife of seventeen years, my comrade, my innermost heart, the mother of my only child—and this ferocious young woman with the burning intelligence, this new erotic charm, a woman I could finally share

my work with and talk to about books and ideas. I began to re-
semble a character in a nineteenth-century novel: solid marriage in one box, lively mistress in another box, and I, the
master magician, standing between them, with the skill and
cunning never to open both boxes at the same time. For several
months I managed to make it work, and I was no longer a mere
magician, I was an aerialist as well, prancing along my high
wire, shuttling between ecstasy and anguish every day, growing
more and more certain that I would never fall.

And then?

December nineteen seventy-four, two days after Christmas.
You fell.

I fell. Sonia did a Schubert recital at the Ninety-second
Street Y that night, and when she came home she told me
she knew.

How did she find out?

She wouldn't say. But all her facts were correct, and I saw
no point in denying them. The thing I remember best about
that conversation was how composed she was—at least until
the end, when she stopped talking. She didn't cry or shout, she
didn't carry on, she didn't punch me or throw things across the
room. You have to choose, she said. I'm willing to forgive you,
but you have to go to that girl right now and break it off. I don't
know what will happen to us, I don't know if we'll ever be the
same again. Right now, I feel as if you've stabbed me in the
chest and ripped out my heart. You've killed me, August.
You're looking at a dead woman, and the only reason I'm going
to pretend to be alive is because Miriam needs her mother. I've

always loved you, I've always thought you were a man with a great soul, but it turns out that you're just another lying shit. How could you have done it, August? . . . Her voice broke then, and she put her face in her hands and started crying. I sat down beside her on the sofa and put my arm around her shoulder, but she pushed me away. Don't touch me, she said. Don't come near me until you've talked to that girl. If you don't come back tonight, don't bother to come back at all—not ever.

Did you come back?

I'm afraid not.

This is getting rather grim, isn't it?

I'll stop if you want me to. We could always talk about something else.

No, keep going. But let's skip ahead, all right? You don't have to tell me about your marriage to Oona. I know you loved her, I know you had a stormy time of it, and I know she left you for that German painter. Klaus Something.

Bremen.

Klaus Bremen. I know how hard it was for you, I know you went through a really bad period.

The alcohol period. Primarily scotch, single-malt scotch.

And you don't have to talk about your troubles with my mother. She's already told me about them. They're finished, and there's no reason to go over them again, is there?

If you say so.

The only thing I want to hear about is how you and Grandma got back together.

This is all about her, isn't it?

It has to be. Because she's the one who isn't here anymore. Nine years apart. But I never turned against her. Regret and remorse, self-contempt, the corrosive poison of uncertainty, those were the things that undermined my years with Oona. Sonia was too much a part of me, and even after the divorce, she was still there, still talking to me in my head—the ever-present absent one, as I sometimes call her now. We were in contact, of course, we had to be because of Miriam, the logistics of shared custody, the weekend arrangements, the summer holidays, the high school and college events, and as we slowly adjusted to our new circumstances, I felt her anger against me turn to a kind of pity. Poor August, the champion of fools. She had men. That goes without saying, *n'est-ce pas?* She was only forty when I walked out on her, still radiant, still the same shining girl she'd always been, and one of her entanglements became quite serious, I think, although your mother probably knows more about it than I do. When Oona waltzed off with her German painter, I was shattered. Your tactful reference to *a bad period* doesn't begin to describe how bad it was. I'm not going to delve into those days now, I promise, but even then, at a time when I was absolutely alone, it never occurred to me to reach out to Sonia. That was nineteen eighty-one. In nineteen eighty-two, a couple of months before your parents' wedding, she wrote me a letter. Not about us, but about your mother, worried that Miriam was too young to be rushing into marriage, that she was about to make the same mistake we did in our early twenties. Very prescient, of course, but your grandmother always had a nose for such things. I wrote back and said she was probably right, but even if she was right, there was nothing we could do about it. You can't meddle with other people's feelings, least of all your own child's, and the truth is that kids learn nothing from their parents' mistakes. We have to leave them alone and let them thrash out into the world to make their own mistakes. That was my answer, and then I concluded the letter with a rather trite remark: The only thing we can do is hope for the best. On the day of the wedding, Sonia walked up to me and said: I'm hoping for the best. If I had to pinpoint the moment when our reconciliation began, I would choose that one, the moment when your grandmother said those words to me. It was an important day for both of us—our daughter's wedding—and there was a lot of emotion in the air—happiness, anxiety, nostalgia, a whole range of feeling—and neither one of us was in a mood for bearing grudges. I was still a wreck at that point, by no means fully recovered from the Oona debacle, but Sonia was going through a hard time as well. She'd retired from singing earlier that year, and as I later found out from your mother (Sonia never shared any secrets with me about her private life), she had recently parted ways with a man. So, on top of everything else, we were both at a low ebb that day, and seeing each other somehow had a consoling effect. Two veterans who'd fought in the same war, watching their child march off to a new war of her own. We danced together, we talked about the old days, and for a few moments we even held hands. Then the party was over, and everyone went home, but I remember thinking when I was back in New York that being with her th day was the best thing that had happened to me in a long time. I never made a conscious decision about it, but one morning about a month later, I woke up and realized that I wanted to see her again. No, more than that. I wanted to win her back. I knew my chances were probably nil, but I also knew that I had to give it a try. So I called.

Just like that? You just picked up the phone and called?

Not without trepidation. Not without a lump in my throat and a knot in my stomach. It was an exact reprise of the first time I'd called her—twenty-seven years before. I was twenty again, a jittery, lovesick juvenile plucking up his courage to call his dream girl and ask her out on a date. I must have stared at the phone for ten minutes, but when I dialed the number at last, Sonia wasn't in. The answering machine clicked on, and I was so rattled by the sound of her voice that I hung up. Relax, I said to myself, you're behaving like an idiot, so I dialed the number again and left a message. Nothing elaborate. Just that I wanted to talk to her about something, that I hoped she was well, and that I would be in all day.

Did she call back—or did you have to try again?

She called. But that didn't prove anything. She had no idea what I wanted to talk about. For all she knew, it might have been about Miriam—or some trivial, practical matter. In any case, her voice sounded calm, a little reserved, but with no edge to it. I told her that I'd been thinking about her and wanted to know how she was. Hanging in there, she said, or words to that effect. It was good to see you at the wedding, I

Yes, she answered, it was a remarkable day, she'd had

a wonderful time. Back and forth we went, a bit tentatively on both sides, polite and cautious, not daring to say much of anything. Then I popped the question: would she have dinner with me one night that week. *Dinner?* As she repeated the word, I could hear the disbelief in her voice. There was a long pause after that, and then she said she wasn't sure, she'd have to think it over. I didn't insist. The important thing was not to come on too strong. I knew her too well, and if I started to push, the odds were that she'd start pushing back. That's how we left it. I told her to take care of herself and said good-bye.

Not such a promising start.

No. But it could have been worse. She hadn't turned down the invitation, she just didn't know if she should accept it or not. Half an hour later, the phone rang again. Of course I'll have dinner with you, Sonia said. She apologized for having hesitated, but I'd caught her with her guard down, and she'd been entirely flustered. So we made our dinner date, and that was the beginning of a long and delicate dance, a minuet of desire, fear, and surrender that went on for more than eighteen months. It took that much time before we started living together, but even though we made it through another twenty-one years, Sonia refused to marry me again. I don't know if you were aware of that. Your grandmother and I lived in sin until the day she died. Marriage would have jinxed us, she said. We'd tried it once, and look what happened to us, so why not take another approach? After struggling so hard to get her back, I was happy to abide by her rules. I proposed to her every year on her birthday, but those declarations were no more than encrypted messages, a sign that she could trust me again, that she could go on trusting me for the duration. There was so much I never understood about her, so much she didn't understand about herself. That second courtship was a tough business, a man wooing his ex-wife, and the ex-wife playing hard to get, not giving an inch, not knowing what she wanted, going back and forth between temptation and revulsion until she finally gave in. It took half a year before we wound up in bed. The first time we made love, she laughed when it was over, collapsing into one of those crazy giggling jags of hers that went on so long I began to grow frightened. The second time we made love, she cried, sobbing into the pillow for more than an hour. So many things had changed for her. Her voice had lost the indefinable quality that had made it her voice, that fragile, crystalline ache of unbridled feeling, the hidden god who had spoken through her—all that was gone now, and she knew it, but giving up her career had been a difficult blow, and she was still coming to terms with it. She taught now, giving private singing lessons in her apartment, and there were many days when she had no interest in seeing me. Other days, she would call in a fit of desperation: Come now, I have to see you now. We were lovers again, probably closer to each other than we'd ever been the first time around, but she wanted to keep our lives separate. I wanted more, but she wouldn't give in. That was the line she wouldn't cross and then, after a year and a half, something happened, and it all suddenly changed.

What was it?

You.

Me? What do you mean, *me*?

You were born. Your grandmother and I took the train to New Haven, and we were there when your mother went into labor. I don't want to exaggerate or sound overly sentimental about it, but when Sonia held you in her arms for the first time, she glanced over at me, and when I saw her face—I'm stumbling here, groping for the right words—her face . . . was illuminated. Tears were rolling down her cheeks. She was smiling, smiling and laughing, and it looked as if she'd been filled with light. A few hours later, after we'd gone back to our hotel, we were lying in bed in the dark. She took hold of my hand and said: I want you to move in with me, August. As soon as we get back to New York, I want you to move in and stay with me forever.

I did it.

You did it. You were the one who got us together again.

Well, at least I've accomplished one thing in my life. Too bad I was only five minutes old and didn't know what I was doing.

The first of many great deeds, with many more to come.

Why is life so horrible, Grandpa?

Because it is, that's all. It just is.

All those bad times with you and Grandma. All the bad times with my mother and father. But at least you loved each other and had your second chance. At least my mother loved my father enough to marry him. I've never loved anyone.

What are you talking about?

I tried to love Titus, but I couldn't. He loved me, but I couldn't love him back. Why do you think he joined that stupid company and went away?

To make money. He was going to put in a year and earn close to a hundred thousand dollars. That's an awful lot of cash for a twenty-four-year-old kid. I had a long talk with him before he left. He knew he was taking a risk, but he thought it was worth it.

He left because of me. Don't you understand that? I told him I didn't want to see him anymore, and so he went off and got himself killed. He died because of me.

You can't think that way. He died because he was in the wrong place at the wrong time.

And I put him there.

You had nothing to do with it. Stop beating yourself up, Katya. It's gone on long enough.

I can't help it.

You've been stuck here for nine months now, and it isn't doing you any good. I think it's time for a change.

I don't want anything to change.

Have you thought about going back to school in the fall?

Off and on. I'm just not sure I'm ready.

It doesn't start for another four months.

I know. But if I want to go back, I have to tell them by next week.

Tell them. If you're not feeling up to it, you can always change your mind at the last minute.

We'll see.

In the meantime, we have to shake things up around here. Does the thought of a trip interest you?

Where would we go?

Anywhere you like, for as long as you like.

What about Mother? We can't just leave her alone.

Her classes end next month. The three of us could go together.

But she's working on her book. She wanted to finish it this summer.

She can write while we're on the road.

The road? You can't ride around in a car. Your leg would hurt too much.

I was thinking more along the lines of a camper. I have no idea what those things cost, but I have a nice chunk of money in the bank. The proceeds from the sale of my New York apartment. I'm sure I could afford one. If not new, then secondhand.

What are you saying? That the three of us drive around in a camper all summer?

That's right. Miriam works on her book, and every day the two of us go off on a quest.

What are we looking for?

I don't know. Anything. The best hamburger in America. We make a list of the top hamburger restaurants in the country and then go around from one to the next and rate them according to a complex list of criteria. Taste, juiciness, size, the quality of the bun, and so on.

If you ate a hamburger every day, you'd probably have a heart attack.

Fish, then. We'll look for the best fish joint in the Lower Forty-eight.

You're pulling my leg, right?

I don't pull legs. Men with bad legs don't do that. It's against our religion.

A camper would be pretty crowded. And besides, you're forgetting one important thing.

What's that?

You snore.

Ah. So I do, so I do. All right, we'll scrap the camper. What about going to Paris? You can see your cousins, practice your French, and gain a new perspective on life.

No thanks. I'd rather stay here and watch my movies.

They're turning into a drug, you know. I think we should cut down, maybe even stop for a while.

I can't do that. I need the images. I need the distraction of watching other things.

Other things? I don't follow. Other than what?

Don't be so dense.

I know I'm dumb, but I just don't get it.

Titus.

But we looked at that video only once—more than nine months ago.

Have you forgotten it?

No, of course not. I think about it twenty times a day.

That's my point. If I hadn't seen it, everything would be different. People go off to war, and sometimes they die. You get a telegram or a phone call, and someone tells you that your son or your husband or your ex-boyfriend has been killed. But you don't see how it happened. You make up pictures in your mind, but you don't know the real facts. Even if you're told the story by someone who was there, what you're left with is words, and words are vague, open to interpretation. We saw it. We saw how they murdered him, and unless I blot out that video with other images, it's the only thing I ever see. I can't get rid of it.

We'll never get rid of it. You have to accept that, Katya. Accept it, and try to start living again.

I'm doing my best.

You haven't stirred a muscle in close to a year. There are other distractions besides watching movies all day. Work, for one thing. A project, something to sink your teeth into.

Like what?

Don't laugh at me, but after looking at all those films with you, I've been thinking that maybe we should write one of our own.

I'm not a writer. I don't know how to make up stories.

What do you think I've been doing tonight?

I don't know. Thinking. Remembering.

As little as possible. I'm better off if I reserve my thinking and remembering for the daytime. Mostly, I've been telling myself a story. That's what I do when I can't sleep. I lie in the dark and tell myself stories. I must have a few dozen of them by now. We could turn them into films. Co-writers, co-creators. Instead of looking at other people's images, why not make up our own?

What kind of stories?

All kinds. Farces, tragedies, sequels to books I've liked, historical dramas, every kind of story you can imagine. But if you accept my offer, I think we should start with a comedy.

I'm not much into laughs these days.

Exactly. That's why we should work on something light—a frothy bagatelle, as frivolous and diverting as possible. If we really put our minds to it, we might have some fun.

Who wants fun?

I do. And you do, too, my love. We've turned into a couple of sad sacks, you and I, and what I'm proposing is a cure, a remedy to ward off the blues.

I launch into a story I sketched out last week—the romantic adventures of Dot and Dash, a chubby waitress and a grizzled short-order cook who work in a New York City diner—but less than five minutes into it, Katya falls asleep, and our conversation comes to an end. I listen to her slow, regular breathing, glad that she's finally managed to conk out, and wonder what time it is. Well past four, probably, perhaps even five. An hour or so until dawn, that incomprehensible moment when the blackness starts to thin out and the vireo who lives in the tree beside my window delivers his first chirp of the day. As I mull over the various things Katya has said to me, my thoughts gradually turn to Titus, and before long I'm inside his story again, reliving the disaster I've been struggling to avoid all night.

Katya blames herself for what happened, falsely linking herself to the chain of cause and effect that ultimately led to his murder. One mustn't allow oneself to think that way, but if I succumbed to her faulty logic, then Sonia and I would be responsible as well, since we were the ones who introduced her to Titus in the first place. Thanksgiving dinner five years ago, just after her parents' divorce. She and Miriam drove down to New York to spend the long weekend with us, and on Thursday Sonia and I cooked turkey for twelve people. Among the guests were Titus and his parents, David Small and Elizabeth Blackman, both painters, both old friends of ours. The nineteen-year-old Titus and the eighteen-year-old Katya seemed to hit it off. Did he die because he fell in love with our granddaughter? Follow that thought through to the end, and you could just as easily blame his parents. If David and Liz hadn't met, Titus never would have been born.

He was a bright boy, I thought, an open-hearted, undisciplined boy with wild red hair, long legs, and big feet. I met him when he was four, and since Sonia and I visited his parents' place fairly often, he felt comfortable around us, treating us not as family friends so much as a surrogate aunt and uncle. I liked him because he read books, a rare kid with a hunger for literature, and when he started writing short stories in his mid-teens, he would send them to me and ask for my comments. They weren't very good, but I was touched that he had turned to me for advice, and after a while he began coming to our apartment about once a month to talk about his latest efforts. I would suggest books for him to read, which he would plow through diligently with a kind of lunging, scattershot enthusiasm. His work gradually improved somewhat, but every month it was different, bearing the marks of whatever writer he happened to be reading at the moment—a normal trait in beginners, a sign of development. Flashes of talent began to glimmer through his ornate, overwritten prose, but it was still too early to judge whether he had any genuine promise. When he was a senior in high school and announced that he wanted to stay in the city to attend college at Columbia, I wrote a letter of recommendation for him. I don't know if that letter made any difference, but my alma mater accepted him, and his monthly visits continued.

He was in his second year when he showed up at that Thanksgiving dinner and met Katya. They made an odd and fetching duo, I thought. The floppy, grinning, arm-waving Titus and the small, slender, dark-haired daughter of my daughter. Sarah Lawrence was in Bronxville, just a short train ride into the city, and Katya stayed with us quite often during her undergraduate days, most weekends in fact, escaping dormitory life for a comfortable bed in her grandparents' apartment and nights out in New York. She now claims that she didn't love Titus, but all during the years they were together, there were dozens upon dozens of dinners at our place, usually just the four of us, and I never felt anything but affection between them. Maybe I was blind. Maybe I took too much for granted, but except for an occasional intellectual disagreement and one breakup that lasted under a month, they struck me as a happy, thriving couple. When Titus came to see me on his own, he never hinted at any trouble with Katya, and Titus was a garrulous boy, a person who spoke whatever was on his mind, and if Katya had called it quits with him, surely he would have mentioned it to me. Or maybe not. It could be that I didn't know him as well as I thought I did.

When he started talking about going off to work in Iraq, his parents went into a tailspin of panic. David, normally the

gentlest and most tolerant of men, screamed at his son and
called him pathologically disturbed, a know-nothing dilet-
tante, a suicidal maniac. Liz wept, took to her bed, and started
gorging herself with heavy doses of tranquilizers. That was in
February last year. Sonia had died the previous November, and
I was in awful shape just then, drinking myself into oblivion
every night, not fit for human contact, out of my mind with
grief, but David was so distraught, he called me anyway and
asked if I would talk some sense into the boy. I couldn't refuse.
I had known Titus for too long, and the fact was that I felt concerned for him as well. So I pulled myself together and did the
best I could—which was nothing, nothing at all.

I had lost touch with Titus after Sonia became ill, and he
seemed to have changed in the intervening months. The talka-
tive, goofy optimist had turned sullen, almost belligerent, and
I knew from the start that my words would have no effect on
him. At the same time, I don't think he was unhappy to see me,
and when he spoke about Sonia and her death, there was true
compassion in his voice. I thanked him for his words, poured
us two glasses of neat scotch, and then led him into the living
room, where we had had so many conversations in the past.

I'm not going to sit here and argue with you, I began. It's
just that I'm a little confused, and I'd like you to clarify some
things for me. Okay?

Okay, Titus said. No problem.

The war has been going on for close to three years now, I
said. When the invasion started, you told me you were against it.
Appalled was the word you used, I think. You said it was a

phony, trumped-up war, the worst political mistake in American history. Am I right, or have I mixed you up with someone else?

You're dead-on. That's exactly how I felt.

We haven't seen much of each other lately, but the last time you were here, I remember you said that Bush should be thrown in jail—along with Cheney, Rumsfeld, and the whole gang of fascist crooks who were running the country. When was that? Eight months ago? Ten months ago?

Last spring. April or May, I can't remember.

Have you changed your thinking since then?

No.

Not at all?

Not one bit.

Then why on earth do you want to go to Iraq? Why participate in a war you detest?

I'm not going there to help America. I'm going for myself.

The money. Is that it? Titus Small, mercenary-at-large.

I'm not a mercenary. Mercenaries carry weapons and kill people. I'm going to drive a truck, that's all. Transporting supplies from one place to another. Sheets and towels, soap, candy bars, dirty laundry. It's a shit job, but the pay is enormous. BRK—that's the name of the company. You sign up for a year, and you come home with ninety or a hundred thousand dollars in your pocket.

But you'll be supporting something you're opposed to. How can you justify that to yourself?

I don't look at it that way. For me, it's not a moral decision. It's about learning something, about starting a new kind of education. I know how horrible and dangerous it is over there, but that's just why I want to go. The more horrible, the better.

You're not making sense.

All my life, I've wanted to be a writer. You know that, August. I've been showing you my wretched little stories for years, and you've been kind enough to read them and give me your comments. You've encouraged me, and I'm very grateful to you for that, but we both know I'm no good. My stuff is dry and heavy and dull. Crap. Every word I've written so far is crap. I've been out of college for close to two years now, and I spend my days sitting in an office, answering the phone for a literary agent. What kind of life is that? It's so fucking safe, so fucking dreary, I can't stand it anymore. I don't *know* anything, August. I haven't *done* anything. That's why I'm going away. To experience something that isn't about me. To be out in the big rotten world and discover what it feels like to be part of history.

Going off to war isn't going to turn you into a writer. You're thinking like a schoolboy, Titus. At best, you'll come back with your head full of unbearable memories. At worst, you won't come back at all.

I know there's a risk. But I have to take it. I have to change my life—*right now.*

Two weeks after that conversation, I climbed into a rented Toyota Corolla and set off for Vermont to spend some time with Miriam. The trip ended with the crash that put me in the hospital, and by the time I was released, Titus had already left for Iraq. There was no chance to say good-bye to him or wish him luck or beg him to reconsider his decision one last time. Such romantic claptrap . . . such childish drivel . . . but the kid was in despair over his ruined ambitions, facing up to the fact that he didn't have it in him to do the one thing he had always wanted to do, and he ran off in an impulsive attempt to redeem himself in his own eyes.

I moved in with Miriam in early April. Three months later, Katya called from New York, sobbing into the phone. Turn on the television, she said, and there was Titus on the evening news, sitting in a chair in some unidentified room with cinder-block walls, surrounded by four men with hoods over their heads and rifles in their hands. The quality of the video was poor, and it was difficult to read the expression on Titus's face. He looked more stunned than terrified, I felt, but apparently he had been beaten, for I could dimly make out what appeared to be a large bruise on his forehead. There was no sound, but over the images the newscaster was reading his prepared text, which went more or less as follows: *Twenty-four-year-old New Yorker Titus Small, a truck driver for the contracting company BRK, was abducted this morning en route to Baghdad. His captors, who have yet to identify themselves with any known terrorist organization, are demanding ten million dollars for his release, as well as the immediate cessation of all BRK activities in Iraq. They have vowed to execute their prisoner if these demands are not met within seventy-two hours. George Reynolds, a spokesman for BRK, said his company is doing everything in its power to ensure Mr. Small's safety.*

Katya arrived at her mother's house the following day, and two nights after that we switched on her laptop and looked at the second and last video shot by the kidnappers, the one that could be seen only on the Internet. We already knew that Titus was dead. BRK had made a substantial offer on his behalf, but as expected (why think the unthinkable when profits are at stake?), they had refused to shut down their operations in Iraq. The slaughter was carried out as promised, precisely seventy-two hours after Titus was torn from his truck and thrown into that room with the cinder-block walls. I still don't understand why the three of us felt driven to watch the tape—as if it were an obligation, a sacred duty. We all knew it would go on haunting us for the rest of our lives, and yet somehow we felt we had to be there with Titus, to keep our eyes open to the horror for his sake, to breathe him into us and hold him there—in us, that lonely, miserable death, in us, the cruelty that was visited on him in those last moments, in us and no one else, so as not to abandon him to the pitiless dark that swallowed him up.

Mercifully, there is no sound.

Mercifully, a hood has been placed over his head.

He is sitting in a chair with his hands tied behind him, motionless, making no attempt to break free. The four men from the previous video are standing around him, three holding rifles, the fourth with a hatchet in his right hand. Without any signal or gesture from the others, the fourth man suddenly brings the blade down on Titus's neck. Titus jerks to his right, his upper body squirms, and then blood starts seeping through the hood. Another blow from the hatchet, this one from behind. Titus's head lolls forward, and by now blood is streaming down all over him. More blows: front and back, right and left, the dull blade chopping long past the moment of death.

One of the men puts down his rifle and clamps Titus's head firmly in his two hands to prop it up as the man with the hatchet continues to go about his business. They are both covered in blood.

When the head is finally severed from the body, the executioner lets the hatchet fall to the floor. The other man removes the hood from Titus's head, and then a third man takes hold of Titus's long red hair and carries the head closer to the camera. Blood is dripping everywhere. Titus is no longer quite human. He has become the idea of a person, a person and not a person, a dead bleeding thing: *une nature morte*.

The man holding the head backs away from the camera, and a fourth man approaches with a knife. One by one, working with great speed and precision, he stabs out the boy's eyes.

The camera rolls for a few more seconds, and then the screen goes black.

Impossible to know how long it has lasted. Fifteen minutes. A thousand years.

I hear the alarm clock ticking on the floor. For the first time in hours, I close my eyes, wondering if it might not be possible to sleep after all. Katya stirs, lets out a little groan, and then rolls onto her side. I consider putting my hand on her back and stroking it for a few seconds but then give up the idea. Sleep is such a rare commodity in this house, I don't want to risk disturbing her. Invisible stars, invisible sky, invisible world. I see Sonia's hands on the keyboard. She's playing something by Haydn, but I can't hear anything, the notes make no sound, and then she swivels around on the stool and Miriam runs into her arms, a three-year-old Miriam, an image from the distant past, perhaps real, perhaps imagined, I can barely tell the difference anymore. The real and the imagined are one. Thoughts are real, even thoughts of unreal things. Invisible stars, invisible sky. The sound of my breath, the sound of Katya's breath. Bedtime prayers, the rituals of childhood, the gravity of childhood. *If I should die before I wake.* How fast it all goes. Yesterday a child, today an old man, and from then until now, how many beats of the heart, how many breaths, how many words spoken and heard? Touch me, someone. Put your hand on my face and talk to me . . .

I can't be sure, but I think I might have dozed off for a while. No more than a few minutes, perhaps only seconds, but suddenly I've been interrupted by something, a sound, I believe, yes, several sounds in fact, a knocking on the door, a faint and persistent knocking, and then I open my eyes and tell Miriam to come in. As the door opens, I can see her face with a certain clarity, and I understand that it's no longer night, that we've come to the cusp of dawn. The world inside my room is gray now. Miriam has already put on some clothes (blue jeans and a baggy white sweater), and the moment she shuts the door behind her, the vireo lets out his first chirp of the day.

What a relief, she whispers, looking at the sleeping Katya. I just checked in on her, and when she wasn't in her bed, I got a little scared.

She came down a few hours ago, I whisper back to her. Another rough night, so we lay in the dark and talked.

Miriam walks over to the bed, plants a kiss on my cheek, and sits down beside me. Are you hungry? she asks.

A little.

Maybe I should start the coffee.

No, sit here and talk to me for a while. There's something I need to know.

About what?

Katya and Titus. She told me she broke up with him before he went away. Is that true? She seems to think he left because of her.

You had so many other things on your mind, I didn't want to bother you with it. Mommy's cancer . . . all those months . . . and then the car accident. But yes, they broke up.

When?

Let me think. . . . Your seventieth birthday was in February, February two thousand and five. Mommy was already sick then. It was just a few months after that. Late spring or early summer.

But Titus didn't leave until the following February, two thousand and six.

Eight or nine months after they broke up.

So Katya is wrong. He didn't go to Iraq because of her.

She's punishing herself. That's what this is all about. She wants to implicate herself in what happened to him, but she really had nothing to do with it. You talked to him before he left. He explained his reasons to you.

And he didn't mention Katya's name. Not once.

You see?

It makes me feel a little better. And also a little worse.

She's coming along now. I can smell it. Bit by bit by bit. The next step is to talk her into going back to school.

She says she's considering it.

Which was out of the question just two months ago.

I grab hold of Miriam's hand and say, I almost forgot. I read some more of your manuscript last night . . .

And?

I think you've nailed it. No more doubts, all right? You're doing a first-rate job.

Are you sure?

I've told a lot of fibs in my day, but I never lie about books.

Miriam grins, aware of the two hundred and fifty-nine secret references buried in that remark, and I grin back at her. Keep on smiling, I say. You look beautiful when you smile.

Only when I smile?

All the time. Every minute of every day.

Another one of your fibs, but I'll take it. She pats me on the cheek and says: Coffee and toast?

No, not today. I think we should go all out this morning. Scrambled eggs and bacon, French toast, pancakes, the whole works.

A farmer's breakfast.

That's it, a farmer's breakfast.

I'll get your crutch, she says, standing up and walking over to the hook on the wall beside my bed.

I follow her with my eyes for a moment, and then I say: Rose Hawthorne wasn't much of a poet, was she?

No. Pretty awful, in fact.

But there's one line . . . one great line. I think it's as good as anything I've ever read.

Which one? she asks, turning to look at me.

As the weird world rolls on.

Miriam breaks into another big smile. I knew it, she says. When I was typing up the quote, I said to myself, He's going to like this one. It could have been written for him.

The weird world rolls on, Miriam.

Crutch in hand, she walks back to the bed and sits down beside me. Yes, Dad, she says, studying her daughter with a worried look in her eyes, the weird world rolls on.

About the Author

PAUL AUSTER is the bestselling author of *Travels in the Scriptorium*, *The Brooklyn Follies*, *Oracle Night*, and *The Book of Illusions*, among many other works. In 2006 he was awarded the Prince of Asturias Prize for Literature and inducted into the American Academy of Arts and Letters. His work has been translated into more than thirty languages. He lives in Brooklyn, New York.